FOOL ME ONCE

JAMIE McFARLANE

D1521133

Copyright © 2014 Jamie McFarlane

All rights reserved.

ISBN: 1499752121
ISBN-13: 978-1499752120

Don't miss any of the stories in
Jamie McFarlane's
PRIVATEER TALES

Rookie Privateer
Fool Me Once
Parley (coming Fall 2014)

CONTENTS

ACKNOWLEDGMENTS

Diane Greenwood Muir, for excellence in editing and fine word-smithery.

My wife, Janet, for carefully and kindly pointing out my poor grammatical habits.

My beta readers. Nancy Higgins Quist for her keen intellect and positive reinforcement. Dave Muir for his careful reading and keen eye. Jeff Rothermel, for solid help with many technical faux-pas and industry insight. Carol Greenwood, my sister, for encouragement.

Patricia Leonardo Cavalieri, cover artist of extraordinary talent.

DARKEST BEFORE DAWN

The cutter was dead in space, no more than a day away from the mining colony, Terrence. I found it ironic that my life would end so close to where it had begun some twenty years ago. The end wasn't hard to accept and I was grateful it would come peacefully.

I looked into the bunk room, turned brig, at my three prisoners, all awake and wanting attention. It was easy to ignore them. For the last eighteen months I had been their prisoner and shown no mercy. They could face their own deaths tied up with full bellies. It was more than they had offered me.

I made my way to the bridge of the thirty meter long ship, kicking debris out of the way. I empathized with the ship. Pirates had used it, abused it, and left it torn and dirty. The pirates had come and gone, using whatever they wanted and then discarding it and me when their abuses made us no longer pretty. I would die with this ship – it seemed fitting.

The armor-glass of the bridge was separated by a spider web of mullions, giving the pilot and co-pilot a nearly 180 degree view of space. I dropped heavily into the pilot's chair on the port side of the bridge and caught a reflection of myself in the glass. I'd been told how pretty I was all my life. It made me laugh humorlessly to see my hollow cheeks and the large scar that cut across my right eye. My once long silky brown, now prematurely white, hair had been cut short and hung limply just to my jawline. Pretty was something that could be stolen, like so many other things.

Liam Hoffen's retreating figure arc-jetted its way back to a nearly identical, albeit better-repaired version of the cutter I sat in. He waited patiently for the airlock to cycle and then let himself into his ship, *Sterra's Gift*.

Hoffen had promised to send me the command codes for the

1

ship I sat in once he was out of weapons range, but I knew better. Men had been making promises to me for far too long. Somehow, it made them feel better to lie. I'd also learned that men were even crueler if I pointed this out.

Sterra's Gift's engines lit up. It turned and accelerated quickly on a new heading. I wondered how long I would be able to survive on this ship. There was plenty of food and the atmo would likely hold for quite some time. Maybe another ship would happen by. *Hope is for someone else*, I thought.

It was completely unexpected when I heard Liam Hoffen's voice hail me through the bridge comms.

"Celina, are you there?"

He hadn't seemed the type to gloat, but nothing really surprised me when it came to men.

"Where else?" I replied.

Hoffen's voice came clear over the bridge's public address, *Transfer full control of cutter to Celina Dontal. Release control by crew of Sterra's Gift from same cutter.*

The disembodied voice of the ship's Artificial Intelligence replied, *Acknowledged, Control transferred to Celina Dontal.*

"That's it. Ship is yours. Happy Sailing!" His voice was cheerful and upbeat.

I was taken aback. The small ember of hope I carried, protected almost entirely by self-loathing, flamed up unexpectedly and threatened to overwhelm me. My voice caught as I responded, "I didn't think you would actually do it."

"Roger that, Celina. Look us up sometime. I bet we will be looking for sharp captains in the future. You know, once I get my business running full tilt." He was clearly enjoying himself.

"Thank you, Liam Hoffen. Someday. Maybe. Dontal out." I closed the communication channel.

I walked to the back of the cutter, to a door just opposite the hallway leading to the airlock. The door opened to an armory just beneath the ship's single turret. I placed the palm of my hand on the panel next to the door which showed a red lock indicator. I felt a vibration from within the door as mechanical bars retracted. The door slowly pushed inward and stopped at five centimeters. I had to press with both hands to open the door enough for me to enter.

The walls of the smaller five by five meter room were covered with shelves. I was very familiar with the room as it was often my duty to load those shelves with slug-thrower ammunition for the turret. When Alexander Boyarov was in an especially vile mood, he'd turn up the gravity in the ship to make it harder for me to load. He'd laugh cruelly and then berate me when I dropped the crates, sometimes using it as an excuse to beat me.

I grabbed a blaster rifle from its cradle on a lower shelf. As soon as my right hand closed around the rifle's grip, the face shield of my vac-suit raised. The AI projected a heads-up display (HUD) onto my retina from my suit's helmet. *Colt 2601-L* displayed on the right side of the HUD, with a translucent gauge that resembled a thermometer showing 100%. The weapon was at full charge.

Full auto, I instructed. The HUD switched from showing three bullets next to the energy meter to the word 'Auto.'

I entered the bunk-room-turned-brig where the captured pirates sat. Upon seeing me enter the room armed, they started talking all at once. Their words were inconsequential.

I considered the three men sitting in front of me, begging for their lives. Olav Peetre was the one who abducted me a year and a half ago. I had known something was fishy but the promise of money lured me into a dangerous situation. It was a pattern I'd repeated since I was twelve and my father had passed away in a mining accident.

Alexander Boyarov was a sadistic brute. He wasn't on the ship in the beginning, but when he showed up, he took a special liking to me and made sure my every waking moment was hell. If I resisted, he would beat me and it could get real ugly.

Jimmy Peng wasn't that bad. He'd never beaten me, and that was something in his favor. If not for Jimmy, my decision would have been relatively easy.

I wasn't a model citizen. To be truthful, I wasn't a citizen at all. Having been a working girl since I was sixteen, I'd never finished school and taken the Mars Competency Test (MCT), a requirement for becoming an Earth Mars Citizen. No, I knew I couldn't really take any moral high ground, even though I had done what was necessary to keep me and my sister alive. What I needed now was the ability to find safe ground, and these three were anything but safe for me.

The chattering died down and only Alexander was stupid, or brave enough to ask, "You crazy bitch, what are you doing? Let us go, you psychotic ..."

It is often said that revenge is not satisfying and not a worthy objective. Watching Alexander Boyarov's head snap back and his hateful spew stop so suddenly was the closest thing to pleasure I'd experienced in years. The look on his face was priceless, bringing a smile.

"It seems I have your attention now," I started.

"I'm gonna break every ..." Alexander Boyarov cut in, recovering from the shock of me firing energy bolts into the wall above his head. The wall diffused the energy bolts without ricochet.

I fired twenty more rounds into the floor near his feet, causing him to jerk them back quickly. His face was red with anger. He was in a dangerous mood at this point. But then, so was I.

"Look ass-hat, I'm not letting you go. I don't want to kill you, but believe me I will. You've got it coming."

"What's your play here, Dontal?" Olav Peetre asked.

"I'll launch a life pod once you're off this boat. We're less than one day from Terrence. I'll make sure someone gets your mayday. You give me trouble and I'll forget about the pod."

"You're not gonna leave us here. What if no one comes for us?" Olav asked.

We went back and forth, but in the end there wasn't much they could do about it. I moved them into the airlock and took a great deal of satisfaction in watching them float out into space. I even waited a solid thirty minutes before launching the life-pod. It was petty, but I enjoyed it.

MISSION DEFINED

My only remaining family was Jenny. The last time I'd seen her we were living together on the space station of the mining colony Terrence. We were saving our money, trying to afford passage back to Mars.

I have only a few memories of Mom. She died after Jenny was born. I used to wear a locket with a picture of her and Dad when they had first been married. They emigrated from Mars to Terrence shortly after that. Dad had it in his mind that they would strike it rich as miners. I was born a couple years after they had gotten set up. Dad was helping work a claim that paid out fairly well. He was putting money away and hoped to actually get his own claim to work.

Mom's accident happened when Jenny was two years old. One day we were a happy family and the next day it was all taken away. It was one of those freak accidents miners call the *Fist of Fate*. A small chunk of space debris, or something that broke loose from a mining operation, moving at extremely high speed, hits you. There is no protection from that. They say, for a few moments you don't even know you're dying. The projectile goes through you so fast, you don't know anything has happened. We were told she didn't suffer, but the older I get, the less I believe that was true.

After Mom's death, Dad pretty much lost it. He didn't hurt us or anything, but our happy life was gone. He worked more and more hours and came home later and later. I soon found out he really wasn't working, but was out spending most of what we had drinking. It passed to me, all of six years old, to raise my little sister. When I was twelve, Dad died in his own accident. This time it wasn't a freak accident. He hadn't been taking care of his vac-suit and simply died for lack of oxygen.

For a few years Jenny and I were handed around between families. The problem was that no one has any money on a mining colony. Food, water and oxygen for two more kids is more than most people could handle. At the age of fourteen I got a waitressing job. I worked twelve hour days and Jenny and I rented the smallest room we could find.

When I was sixteen, I finally gave in to the pressure and was turned out as a prostitute. I would like to say it was terrible, but that was only part of it. I hated myself for what I was doing and I hated lying to Jenny, but we had actually started to save money. Resisting the drugs was what I struggled with the most. It would have been so easy to give in, but I wasn't about to repeat my old man's sins and give up on my family. One single rock shouldn't have the ability to end so many lives. Jenny depended on me. I was willing to give up myself, but not her.

That was, of course, until Olav Peetre lured me onto this very ship. I had to get back to Terrence and find Jenny. With a ship, we had a chance to escape. We could make our way to Puskar Stellar on Mars. Surely there, we would be able to eke out a better life.

I had assets if I could keep control of them. Liam Hoffen had allowed me to grab two cases from the pirate warehouse as my personal plunder. Well, technically, it was six cases and he chose two I could keep. He let the others: Olav, Alexander and Jimmy do the same. I wasn't sure what was in them, but now I had eight cases and a brick of platinum from my deal with Hoffen. He said the platinum was worth twenty thousand Mars credits (m-creds). I thought the brick felt a little light, but he wasn't too far off.

First things first, however. I needed to locate Jenny. She was fourteen when I'd been taken and I desperately hoped she had been able to take care of herself. She'd be sixteen now. I wasn't sure how to explain what happened. She was going to be beyond mad. But that didn't matter. We were family and we'd get past it.

For the last year and a half I hadn't even had access to the network, one of the most unsettling aspects of my captivity. I realized that I could now see all of the communications I'd missed.

Open communication's queue. Prioritize messages from Jenny.

6

If I'd been paying attention, I would have noticed the small throbbing glow in my vac-suit's HUD a lot earlier. The minute I'd gained control of the cutter, my AI had started all sorts of interfacing, including automatic retrieval of pending messages. AI functions were something all spacers took for granted. It was common for an AI to queue up communications for short periods of time while in flight, because the ship's engines could cause interference. Otherwise, communications arrived at the speed of light. From one side of the solar system to the other this could be as long as three hours. I'd been out of reach for eighteen months.

A list of more than a hundred communications filled my screen. I made my way back to the pilot's seat and grabbed a reading pad. It wasn't strictly necessary, but sometimes the HUD gave me a headache. I didn't need to instruct my AI to move the projected list onto the reading pad, I had been training it since I was very young and this was a common enough event for me.

I decided to start from the bottom of the list and move up.

Cel. You didn't come home last night. I have to run to school, see you this afternoon. TTFN – Jenny

Hey. It's getting late. Let me know what's up. Oh and they're saying there's a new family setting up on claim eight hundred oh forty two. Misty says she got a look at the new boy and he looks delicious.

Cel, I'm getting worried. Why won't you message me back?

Tears streamed down my cheeks at the sound of her voice. She was so innocent and happy. I didn't want to continue because she was never be able to reach me and I couldn't take the eventual rejection I knew was coming. Jenny continued sending several messages each day, ranging from anger, to apology, to fearful speculation. They changed from hope to a weary acceptance after a couple of weeks.

Hi Cel – I hope you're able to hear this wherever you are. I miss you. I was able to get a job at Magees' Diner. It's a little weird. I'm basically taking Mom's and your old job. The pay is not very good. I hope I can keep the apartment. I still have most of our savings.

Cel, had a guy grab my ass today. I told him off, but he just stared at me. Magee didn't even seem to care. She said it comes with the job. It made me feel sad, especially after I thought about what you had to do for us. I miss you.

Cel, I moved in with Misty and her family. We have to share a bed but she's being a real pal. I pay rent and have to get my own food and oh-two, but at least I can make it. I love you.

The messages continued and became more and more spread out in time. I continued to listen. The last message I received was startling.

Cel, I can't take it anymore. Where's this leading to? What am I doing on this station? I'm barely surviving. There's a family trading ship, Domiva's Grace, docked up this week. I was talking to one of the family members, a boy. He said they might have room for me to ride back with them to Puskar Stellar. It's what we always wanted, Cel. I will have to give them all of our savings. I'm really thinking about doing it. I wish you were here. Love you.

It was the last message from Jenny.
Open channel to Jenny on Terrence.
Jennifer Dontal is not within communication range. Would you like to send a message?

Jenny, it's a long story, but I'm finally safe. Please tell me where you are. I need to know you are safe. Love you.

Open channel to Magee on Terrence.
"This is Magee. Celina? Is that you girl?" I was close enough to the Terrence station that the communication delay was minimal.
"Hi Magee, yes, of course. How are you?" I wasn't sure how to handle the conversation.
"We sure have been worried about you. You must be close,

8

where have you been?" I figured it was natural that she was curious, but I really didn't have the energy to explain.

"I'm sorry Magee, I'm looking for Jenny. It's a long story."

"She quit two months ago, haven't seen her since. She said something about signing on with a family trading ship. I don't remember the name. I told her to be careful. Sometimes those ships are dangerous, especially for a young woman, if you get my meaning."

"Uh, sure. So you haven't heard from her since then?"

"Not at all. So where'd you say you've been?" she asked.

"Thank you, Magee. I really appreciate what you did for all of us." I wasn't about to get into it with her.

"Okay, dear. Stop in if you're looking for work. You Dontals have always been good help."

I ended the communication. Magee wasn't much help. Maybe Misty would know something. The last time I had seen her she was thirteen, a year younger than Jenny.

Open channel with Misty, Jenny's friend. I hoped that would be enough. I couldn't remember her last name but I was hoping my AI would be able to find a reference somewhere in my history.

"Now you show up?" Misty sounded angry and I felt like I'd entered the middle of a conversation.

I wasn't about to get into it with her either. "Misty, I need to find Jenny. Do you know where she is?"

"You can't keep doing this to her, you abandoned her."

"Had my own problems, Misty. I need to find her."

"She's gone. She got a ride from a family trading ship and took off. I haven't heard from her and she's not leaving messages."

"What ship? What family?"

"I don't remember."

"Was it *Domiva's Grace*? She mentioned that in a message she sent me."

"I think so. You hurt her bad, Celina." Apparently Misty wasn't done with me.

"I know. Bad things happened. Thank you for helping her. I owe you." I didn't know what to say.

"She was my friend. I'd do anything for her. What are you going to do?"

"I'm going to find her, no matter the cost."

"I think she's on Puskar Stellar."

"Why do you think that? I thought you hadn't heard from her."

"I haven't, but I know that the family trader ship was eventually headed to Puskar Stellar."

"Thanks Misty. That's a big help."

"I'm scared for her, Celina. She wouldn't just stop talking to me. We're best friends."

"Stuff happens, Misty. I'll find her."

"Are you coming back here?"

"Nothing there for me."

"Take me with you."

"Sorry. Wish I could. I gotta go."

Calculate fastest transit to Puskar Stellar. Verify oh-two crystals and water for one person. Include twelve hour breaks for communication relay. The AI showed that I had more than enough oh-two and even though I'd have to be careful with water, I would make it.

Execute transit plan.

The ship shuddered under the acceleration of the three large engines. This ship was in pretty bad shape and the trip would be hard on it. I didn't really care, as long as it got me closer to Jenny.

The g-force was uncomfortable while under hard burn, as the gravity in the ship had to run at 1.5 gravity. I'd been living between .4 and .6 for a long time and my body wasn't used to the stress. Sixty percent, or .6 g, was the lowest safe level for long term exposure, but try telling that to pirates. My body would have to adjust. I simply felt weary.

The ship I was sailing was a General Astral cutter and served as a multi-purpose tool for the Navy as well as large corporations. It worked well as a light cargo hauler, but wasn't big enough to be considered a freighter. It was, however, capable of getting supplies to remote locations quickly. The ship was also great for long distance patrols. With bunk rooms empty of cargo, it could haul a crew of up to ten comfortably for a few weeks. Finally, the cutter had teeth in the form of a large slug-throwing turret that provided 360 degrees of horizontal freedom and better than 180 degrees of vertical freedom. Several different missile packages could be outfitted, depending on the mission.

Optimal capability and current status are often two very different things. The cutter was currently only able to accelerate at about 60%. The primary head, where the shower was located, didn't work at all and the secondary head was making some bad noises. I could be in a real pinch if it stopped working over the next twelve days. If I encountered pirates, I had no idea how to operate the turret and there were no missiles attached.

The bridge was in decent shape compared to the rest of the ship. It was configured with two large pilot chairs at the front on a slightly lower level. On the upper level were two stations where support crew sat and helped with watch duties.

I chose the port side pilot's chair. It was in the best shape of the two and as a result was also the cleanest. Space-faring ships pretty much sailed themselves when not in combat. Even then, the ship's AI did most of the work, translating the pilot's gestures and commands into actual adjustments to the ship's acceleration and attitude.

I slumped into the chair and looked out into space. It was a uniquely satisfying moment. I'd finally escaped the Red Houzi pirates. The weight of dread was slowly seeping out of my body and I relaxed. If Jenny were with me, everything would have been perfect. I'd learned the hard way that control was an illusion. You had to enjoy the small moments when you got them.

I awoke in the chair, with no idea how long I'd been asleep. A trip to the secondary head reminded me that I was living on a pirate ship - a group primarily dominated by young men. That is to say, it was completely disgusting. I decided to look for cleaning supplies, although expecting to find them seemed a little ridiculous. Most of the men, or women for that matter, in Red Houzi wouldn't know which end of a cleaning brush was the business end. Unfortunately for me, I had often been assigned the lowly task of cleaning up.

To my surprise, I located a brush and a small amount of abrasive cleaning powder. It wasn't enough to scrub the floor, but the head and sink could be attended to. For once, I'd be the only one using this room and could clean up my own mess.

I grabbed a meal ration bar. I'd grown accustomed to eating a single bar each day, which was only six hundred calories. Between my normally small size and my current emaciated form, only a few calories were required to support my body's forty-five kilograms. I was a little concerned that I'd lost ten kilos over the last year and a half. The most dramatic change, however, was that my previously brown hair had turned a silvery white.

I resolved to eat two meal bars every day. I was too weak to do much exercise, but I had a new lease on life. I had a reason to live.

Returning to the bridge, I used my AI to look up ways to add strength that could be done in a small space. I found an endless supply of beautiful women jumping and dancing to music. I finally settled on one of the easier routines and although I couldn't keep up, I did my best. After only a few minutes, I was exhausted. I resolved to increase movement at least twice a day. Between this and the increased gravity, I should be in better shape by the time I reached Mars.

I turned on some light Earth jazz from the early twenty first century and relaxed. It reminded me of my mom. She was into music from this era and it helped me remember her, and even Dad, from when times were better. "I'm going to find Jenny and we'll be a family again," I promised.

Send communication to Domiva's Grace. Audio only.

Greetings to whoever receives this on Domiva's Grace. I'm Celina Dontal. I recently received information that my sister Jennifer Dontal booked passage from Terrence to Puskar Stellar sometime around 498.02.01. I'm unable to contact Jenny and was hoping you would reply with information about her passage. I'm her legal guardian and am simply trying to locate or contact her.

It was a long shot. They might balk at replying, as legally, they shouldn't have transported a minor without consent of her legal guardian. I might have been declared unfit or dead or something, but I didn't think it would hurt to use a little leverage.

I waited up for the next communication relay, hoping for word from *Domiva's Grace*. Under normal circumstances they should have received my message within an hour if they were on Earth, Mars, or even any of the mining colonies in the main belt between Mars and Jupiter.

Sleep came easily again that night, even though I had some anticipation about receiving a message back from *Domiva's Grace*. I awoke refreshed in the port-side pilot's chair. I was interested in working on my routine, which would be focused on finding Jenny and rebuilding my body. The Red Houzi had taken too much from me and I would get it back.

I found an AI search service to scour public records, looking for information on Jennifer Dontal, aged sixteen. It would cost more than I had in the account Jenny and I shared, but once I'd seen the account hadn't had any activity over the last two months, I didn't care. It'd been nearly emptied with one big transfer to *Domiva's Grace*. I wondered again why they hadn't gotten back to me.

It was frustrating. I had goods worth, hopefully, a small fortune, but no ability to sell them. I decided to do what I could - become acquainted with what I had in my possession. I needed to know exactly what I had so when the time came, I could research prices and know which items would sell quickly. I'd learned the hard way that not knowing the value of something was a sure way to get cheated.

I emptied one of the bunk rooms of all the debris left behind by the pirates. It was still dirty, but at least it lacked junk. Eight large cases of loot from the Red Houzi base took me the better part of three days to final inventory, arrange similar items, and repack. Each case was about a meter wide and tall and about a meter and a half long. The box I felt had the most promise held stacks of gold and silver coins and assorted jewelry. It might be tricky selling some of the larger pieces of jewelry, since they were likely registered as stolen. One bridge at a time.

On the fourth day, while I was working on valuing some of the smaller art pieces in case number four, I heard a chirp from my AI. Initially it startled me, not having received messages for so many months. My heart leapt with the possibility of a message from Jenny.

Play message.

A shiver ran up my spine as I heard Alexander Boyarov's voice.

Dontal, you crazy bitch. You better be looking over your shoulder because I'm coming for you. The Captain blames you for the raid on the base and is sending me after you. I had a little chat with Magee and I'm afraid the old gal isn't going to make it. I didn't know you had a little sister so I did a little checking around and I know right where she is. She sounds like a sweet little thing, I can't wait to break her in. Don't worry, I'll record it for you. Why don't you turn that ship around and meet me back here at Terrence. I can't promise I'll take it easy on you, but maybe I'll forget about your little sister.

I should have expected the message, but I'd pushed him out of my mind. The Captain he was referring to was someone I'd never met, but I knew he was higher up in the Red Houzi hierarchy. Boyarov could be bluffing, but I had no doubt that if he and I met again it wouldn't go well for me.

It was even more urgent than before that I find Jenny.

TRIP TO MARS

After five days of sailing toward Puskar Stellar on Mars, I finally heard from *Domiva's Grace*. The message was short and to the point. They'd never transported anyone by the name of Jennifer Dontal, period. If I had any further questions, I was to contact their legal counsel on Earth. It was a terrible letdown. It was odd that they referred me to their legal counsel, however. I hadn't pushed that hard. It felt like they were hiding something, although that could just be wishful thinking on my part. I was currently in no position to push the issue.

Life aboard the ship became routine after that. I continued to exercise and pushed myself to eat twice a day. I'd put on at least three kilos and my cheeks had lost some of their hollow look. My hair wasn't as thin as it had been at the start of the journey, but the silver color appeared to be permanent. I was happy to see the muscles in my legs and arms filling out, though I was still very thin. It would take time.

On day six, the ship broke from hard burn, spun a graceful 180 degrees on its vertical axis, and fired the engines back up. One of the disadvantages of this ship's design was that slowing down required the ship to be pointed away from its eventual destination. I would have enjoyed watching Mars grow through the armor glass, but it wasn't possible. Part of my HUD showed the approach, but I felt a little cheated.

For the first time in my life I saw multiple ships within range of my own. At first, I worried that Alexander Boyarov had arrived before me or that some other Red Houzi ship was on to me. But they all kept to their original courses and sailed by.

When I was three hundred thousand kilometers from Mars, my ship flipped over again and the deceleration dropped off considerably. The planet was breathtaking with its purplish glow. Large numbers of ships of all sizes were approaching and leaving from all points around its perimeter. Mars was the biggest object in space I'd ever seen.

The ship I was in was probably unregistered and possibly even listed as stolen. Fearing Red Houzi's reach, I needed to be careful. It would eventually need to be abandoned, but first I planned to land at Puskar Stellar. It was the main trading hub on Mars and there was no registration requirement for ships.

Negotiate with Puskar Stellar and find a landing site that doesn't require upfront fees.

I wasn't holding a reading pad so my AI used the sound system on the bridge to communicate.

There are five landing sites that do not require upfront fees. Three require bond and proof of ownership.

My AI had anticipated a problem I hadn't considered. I picked up a reading pad.

Show remaining two.

My pad showed a top view map of Puskar Stellar. The city was huge, fifteen kilometers on one side and twenty-three on the other. Glowing outlines indicated the two public landing sites. Both were located on the edge of a part of town called the Open Air District. I was thrilled. That was our original destination when Jenny and I planned to come here in the first place.

The Open Air District was known throughout the solar system as a place where free trade took place. It had no taxation system beyond that which was paid to rent real estate. Goods and services weren't taxed by the Mars Protectorate or even by Puskar Stellar. If you couldn't buy it here then it probably didn't exist.

Negotiate landing permission on Budget Park #1.

I had no idea which lot might be better, but ultimately I didn't expect to keep the ship. Red Houzi would find it - and me - soon enough.

My pad showed a confirmation of permission.

Plot course to land at Budget Park #1.

My AI returned a positive chirp letting me know it had heard, understood, and would act accordingly.

Mars continued to grow in my vision as I approached. It seemed impossibly large. I'd never been so close to an actual planet and the scale was incredible.

Turret lockdown permission required.

I expected this. Many space stations required turrets be locked down and Puskar Stellar was no different.

Accept.

I would land by 1800 universal which translated to 0200 local time for Puskar Stellar. In space, everyone worked with universal time, but the planets used local time to help line up with when the Sun would shine on the surface. It was a weird concept to me. Out on mining colonies, the sun was a nice reference point, but it had nothing to do with the time of day. The good news was the Martian day was still about twenty-four hours, so once I lined my sleep pattern up with local time, I wouldn't have to adjust to a different day length.

Puskar Stellar was in a night cycle, so activity should have been at a minimum, but the number of ships landing and taking off was incredible. There were thousands and thousands of ships of all sizes going in all different directions. You couldn't have convinced me to take the stick and fly manually, I wouldn't have the first idea how to navigate. How these ships weren't hitting each other was beyond me.

The lights of Puskar Stellar were beautiful and numerous. They spread out for hundreds of kilometers in all directions. As the ship approached the landing site, I could make out buildings and colorful tent tops.

PUSKAR STELLAR

At the bottom of my ship's ramp, a chubby little man dressed in a poorly fitting pair of jeans that weren't up to the task of covering his belly, met me. Without suspenders, his pants would never have been able to stay up. I hoped the stains on his white sleeveless shirt were just grease, but I didn't know for certain.

My face-shield was up, as was common practice when exiting a ship. It wasn't until I noticed he wasn't wearing a vac-suit at all that it occurred to me we were standing in a pressurized environment. Strike that. Mars wasn't just pressurized, it had an oxygen-nitrogen mixture over its entire surface, as did Earth. It was just weird. It took some effort for me to lower the face-shield and allow my helmet to fall back between my shoulder blades.

Having had no access to a suit cleaner or a shower for what felt like decades, I would never have bet against myself for "worst smell," but I think this little guy could actually give me a run for my money.

The man's stare was unabashed as he looked me up and down, his eyes coming to rest somewhere below my chin. I took a little pride in this because, twelve days ago, I doubt even this man would have thought I was much to look at.

"It's two hundred a day, starting today, no matter how much of a day you use. Clamps are already locked so there's no getting out of it. How many days you planning on being here, darling?" His voice was low and raspy, like he had swallowed sand.

"At least a week," I answered.

"I couldn't help but notice your ship's not registered." He finally raised his eyes to look at my face.

Damn. That was the point of landing here, supposedly they didn't check.

"Is that going to be a problem?" I asked, pouting my lips.

"I suspect we can work something out," he answered, his gravelly voice conveying the lust he clearly felt.

I placed my hand under his chin and stroked it lightly. "Well, we'll just have to see, won't we?" I punctuated by tapping my index finger on his nose. It never ceased to amaze me how disgusting little men would believe that someone might be interested in them. I gave him a smile that communicated amusement at his advance.

"Is there anywhere a girl could get a shower?" I asked, changing subjects.

A broad grin spread across his face. "I bet we have something for that. Name's Benny. You need anything around here, you ask for me. Got it?"

"Call me Lena."

Benny led me through the lot to a centralized building. The lot was surrounded by twenty meter high gray walls. Benny showed me where the semi-private showers were and pointed out a suit freshener.

"Not too many 'round here wear vac-suits. Might stand out if you do." Benny wasn't making any move to leave the shower room. No doubt he thought some sort of payment was due in advance.

I turned away and started peeling off my vac-suit. The skin tight suit-liner drew his greasy little eyes to my body. I'd been with much worse, but whether Benny knew it or not, that wasn't where this was headed. His breath caught in his throat as I wiggled out of the suit.

"Benny, sweetie, I'm exhausted and have been sailing for weeks. Would you be a dear and run my things through the freshener?" I used my sweet damsel voice.

I pulled my suit liner down to my waist, exposing my breasts only slightly. With my back still turned to him, I wiggled it over my non-existent hips. The vac-suit and liner puddled at my feet. I walked out of my clothes into a shower stall without turning to see if Benny was doing as I asked.

"Uh, sure, Doll, let me get those."

"You're a prince. How about you toss your shirt in there too. A girl likes a clean man, you know." It was a small public service I was performing.

The hot water felt luxurious, as did the scent of Martian air. It didn't smell of machinery but had a slightly sweet smell. Washing the grime off felt so wonderful. I was lost in the enjoyment of it when I heard Benny's raspy voice outside the stall.

"Uh, I put your clothes on a bench out here, and I, uh, washed my shirt too." There was hope in his voice. It was time to crush his dreams.

"You are too good to me." I turned off the water and leaned out of the door to grab my suit liner. I allowed Benny to get a small peek, but not too much. It wouldn't do to make him think I was easy. He could deal with a little rejection, no doubt he'd lived with it his entire life.

"Where's a girl get something to eat around here?" I asked. I had forty m-creds in my account. It should cover a single meal but not much more.

"I like to eat at Fortieth Street Diner," Benny offered.

"Join me?"

He thought for a moment. "Sure Doll, I'll even buy."

Oh, this was too easy. I might feel guilty at some point.

Outside the ship-lot, the twenty meter tall walls were constructed out of red bricks. I had to touch the brick, as the material was so foreign to me. Plastic or steel were the building materials of space stations, not bricks. I giggled at the feel of the rough structure. It wasn't completely a show for Benny, but I also knew that his perception of me as a bubble-head wasn't necessarily a bad idea.

Wide walkways between the buildings were mostly one or two levels and the streets had stylized lights hanging from tall, regularly spaced posts.

"This is the Italian district," Benny, the tour guide, informed me. "They say these are reproductions of actual buildings from Italy, on Earth. Look, there, at the streets, those are all real bricks.

If we got one thing here on Mars, it's clay. You should see those little mason bots go. They can put up a building in less than a week. It's not a real big deal since they just build 'em from pictures, but I think it's pretty neat. Bet you never seen anything like that where you come from."

I hooked my arm into his. He wasn't so bad and at least his shirt was clean. The streets weren't particularly empty and we walked from one pool of light to the next. There were small groups of people who mostly looked to be wrapping it up for the night.

"This time of night is as quiet as it ever gets here. In ten hours or so it's really hopping. All the vendors will have their goods out on tables up and down the streets. You'll hardly be able to walk through here. About ten at night, the entertainment folks take over. Best bands on the planet come here to play, then it folds up at two in the morning. We start the next day with the food vendors in the morning."

"Ten? Two? What are you talking about?"

"Oh baby, we don't go on military here. Ten is 2200 or 1000 and two is 0200 and 1400. You get used to it."

Dinner was good, although I couldn't eat much. My stomach still wasn't used to getting much food each day. Benny continued to fill me in on the details of life on Puskar Stellar. He remained a gentleman through dinner and walked me back to the ship. Somewhere along the line I'd switched from being a mark to being a real person to him.

"You show all the girls this good of a time on their first date?" I asked him.

"Nah, you're just the first one to be nice to me."

I leaned over and kissed him on his head. "You're sweet Benny. You around tomorrow?"

"Always am."

"Take me out to see a band?" I asked.

"Seriously?" He asked, confused. "I thought you were just trying to get some free rent on the ship."

"Tell you what. You clean those pants, take a shower and put on a decent looking shirt and we'll go on a proper date. Heck, you pick the spot and I'll even buy." I was bluffing. Benny had been a good guy, but there was no way I paying for anything.

"You're on, Doll. Benny'll take care of you good." I liked his raspy voice, but when he leaned in, he smelled awful.

IF THE SHOE FITS, BUY IT IN EVERY COLOR

I woke up the next day at 1400 local. I loved how I smelled, or more accurately, didn't smell, and ran my hands through my hair. It felt good to be clean.

Locate closest mineral exchange. Find current value of platinum.

There are five mineral exchanges within two kilometers of current location. Platinum is trading at forty-two point two oh nine per gram, the ship answered from the bridge.

I picked up a reading pad. I needed to remember to bring one with me so I wouldn't have to raise my face shield while I was out. I had no clothing other than my vac-suit. It was one more item I'd need to take care of.

The five hundred gram bar of platinum that Liam Hoffen traded for my cooperation while he took over the Red Houzi base got strapped to my midsection beneath my breasts. It wouldn't do to lose it. A stack of gold coins worth six thousand m-creds went in a pouch beneath my belt. My first day out would be my safest. Once word got out that I carried valuables, trouble would find me.

I closed the ship's door and walked down the ramp, hoping I'd distracted Benny enough the night before so he hadn't put the word out on me yet. He'd given away his intent when he mentioned that my ship was unregistered. Dinner and the promise of a date should buy me a couple more days. Money makes people unpredictable, but I'd given myself the best shot I could.

My eyes hurt from the sun. Until last night I'd never been outside a pressurized environment. The sweet smell of the air was intoxicating, but the brightness was blinding. I instinctively held my hand up to cover my eyes. It helped. The next thing I noticed was the noise filtering over the top of the high walls of the Budget Park. I could tell I was in for a lot of new experiences.

Exiting onto the brick streets, I was surprised by the transformation. Benny's description was, if anything, too modest. Where it had been mostly empty the night before, now there were tables and tents neatly arranged up and down the entire street. The spectacle continued as far as I could see.

The light filtering through the colored tent awnings was beautiful. There was a cart loaded with flowers of every possible size and shape. Children were running down the street wearing shorts and t-shirts, and women were in dresses and skirts. Men wore jeans and suits, and though a few people wore their vac-suits, we were very much in the minority. I needed to fix that. I didn't want to stand out.

I chastised myself for getting lost in it all. I was carrying more wealth than I'd ever owned and hoped I could use it to find my sister. I needed to focus. I wasn't safe and didn't know where danger would come from first.

My reading pad gave me directions to my first stop - Punjay's Pawn. It didn't sound like a place that would buy platinum, but they might bite on the gold coins. The pawn shop was cleaner than I'd expected. The tables outside were filled with displays of jewelry, knives, small electronic devices, and some real books.

Inside the store, a young, dark-skinned man with black, loose curly hair stood behind a glass counter containing more expensive looking jewelry on one side and a handful of pistols on the other. He offered a quick smile as I approached.

"Welcome to Punjay's. What can I help you find? Perhaps a beautiful ring for your long, lovely fingers?"

"Are you Punjay?" I asked.

"Oh no, but I am his nephew, Samsir. Whatever you need, I will help you."

"Okay, Samsir. What can you tell me about this?" I handed him one of the twelve gold coins I carried, already fully aware that the value was close to five hundred m-creds.

Samsir placed the coin on a soft gray scan pad on the counter. He turned a reading pad around so I could see what it had gleaned.

"Very nice. It is a gold dollar coin from early Earth history. I will give you two hundred creds for this."

"If I sold you that coin for two hundred it would be the last coin you would see. We both know it's worth at least six hundred."

"No, Punjay would fire poor Samsir if I gave away so much of his money. But you seem to be an educated woman and maybe Samsir has underestimated the value of your coin. Perhaps you would consider two hundred fifty?"

"Well Samsir, I guess Punjay will not need to be upset with you. I will take no less than five hundred for my coin and it seems you aren't interested. I appreciate your time."

I picked up the coin and slid it into a small pouch on my suit and turned to walk out. The coins were worth five hundred, but even though I couldn't expect someone to give me full retail, I wasn't ready to take a fifty percent loss. There was time to visit a few more shops.

I was barely outside when I heard the baritone voice of an older man behind me. "Young lady, please come back and visit with me. My boy, Samsir, is under a lot of pressure."

A man in a long, off-white robe stood in the doorway. The dark skin of his face was framed by a neatly trimmed grey beard and a necklace of satiny black rocks hung from his neck. He wore a gentle smile that didn't quite reach his eyes.

"With whom do I have the pleasure of speaking?" I asked.

"Punjay Gowda, and this is my humble establishment." He spread out his hands to indicate the store.

I followed him back inside and Samsir was nowhere to be seen. We didn't stop at the front counter, but walked past into an office overlooking the main room of his shop. He motioned for me to sit in one of two ornate red high-backed chairs.

"May I see the coin?" he asked.

I handed it to him.

"It is a beauty. My best number is three hundred fifty. I must have room to make a profit." He sounded very convincing.

"We're getting closer, Mr. Gowda, but you need to know I'm looking for a business partner, not a one night stand. How about you give me your best number now or I will just move on. You know better than I do, I will eventually find someone to give me a fair price. I think that should be you, don't you agree?"

"It would seem I should know your name if we are to be business partners," he said smoothly.

"My friends call me Lena."

"Well Lena, my dear, I assume you have more than one of these coins and now you certainly have stirred my curiosity. It would seem coins of this nature might be in the company of other similarly interesting items. Would that be the type of partner you are looking for?"

"You have a fanciful imagination, Mr. Gowda. Let me state that if I were able to find someone who could help me with this coin, then that would be a good start."

Punjay Gowda held the coin up and pretended to inspect it in-depth, trying to divine some new hidden value. We both knew it was a show. His AI had already told him what he could expect to sell it for, its break-even point, and had probably offered different thresholds for twenty, thirty, forty and fifty percent returns. He was just buying himself some time.

"Okay, Lena. I'll bite. Forty-seven fifty for the entire dozen."

I was a little startled to find he knew I was carrying that many coins. It was a good price. The way I figured it, he would make twenty percent. He was sending a message by tipping his hand about his awareness of the other eleven coins.

"Immediate transfer?" I asked.

"Yes."

"Agreed."

"Anything else you wish to discuss?" he asked. By now, I had no doubt he knew I had something strapped to my chest. If he was willing to work at twenty percent, I was willing to lay my cards on the table.

"How are you set for funds? Will you work at twenty percent for precious metal, ninety-two percent pure?"

"How much?"

"You would need an additional eighteen thousand."

"If it pans out, yes," he answered.

"Immediate transfer as well?"

"Yes."

I unzipped my suit-liner far enough down the front to unstrap the small platinum bar and placed it on the table.

"Ahh. Platinum. You are asking eighteen thousand?"

"I am."

Standing outside a few minutes later, I considered my accomplishments. If I didn't settle anything else that day, liquidating those assets was enough. I could now move to my next objective - trying to fit in. For that, I needed to do some people watching.

I consulted my map, even though I knew it would mark me as a tourist. I was no longer carrying anything of any value, so my risk was low. There was a concentration of restaurants a few blocks away and I was hungry.

Small round tables with umbrellas, littered the restaurant district I'd discovered. Subtle differences in table size and umbrella style or color made it obvious which tables belonged to which cafés. It was hard to imagine that this hadn't been here last night or that the décor wasn't anything but original. The building's walls looked like they had been there for centuries and the weather-worn look of the bricks in the street gave that same feeling of age. I felt completely out of place in my vac-suit and poorly maintained hair.

If the waiter noticed, he was polite enough not to say anything, and I was grateful for that small kindness. I didn't recognize anything on the menu. I needed to choose a persona. Who would I be? What would my story be? I scanned the crowd for women my age and tried to figure out who they were and what they might be doing. The first women who caught my attention was in a flowery dress with bright red shoes. She had matching glossy red paint on her lips and long flowing blonde hair. There were bags on the ground next to her, so she was obviously out shopping. A thin flat golden wire ran along her cheek from her ear to just in front of her eye. I wasn't sure how it was attached but it was an HUD of some sort. She sat there chatting loudly into it and drinking from an impossibly small cup of something. Clearly, a woman with few problems on her mind. It wouldn't be my first choice, but I thought I could pull it off, if necessary. She was mesmerizing to watch. The world owed her and she knew it.

The waiter caught my attention, "Madame, have you decided?" He spoke with an accent I didn't recognize.

"I'm new in town and not sure what is good to eat. Would you make a recommendation?" The waiter was at least forty years old and I knew, being a man, he couldn't resist the request. His face lit up.

"Oh, then let Moreno take care of you, if you please. Such a beautiful woman is a joy to serve. The chef has a delightful antipasto with a delicious vino cheese. We would follow that with a small serving of our fettuccini noodles with olive oil and to top it off, a pastry made right here by our very own chef." He beamed at me.

"That sounds wonderful, Moreno." I was a little afraid it would be too much, but I needed to spend time here. Moreno bustled off, only to return with a small glass of a white bubbly drink.

"d'Asti for the lady," he announced and waited for me to take a drink. I obliged and found it to be sweet and alcoholic. I smiled in acknowledgement.

The next woman I saw was quite the opposite of the flowery woman with red shoes. Dressed entirely in gray, she wore long pants and a coat. Her hair was pulled back severely and she punctuated her conversation with sharp movements. She was interesting, but a business woman was not what I was looking for.

Moreno brought out a small plate of cheese with thin pieces of meat.

"Your antipasto." He bustled off without waiting to see if I enjoyed it or not.

By the time I'd finished my meal and a delicious cup of coffee, I was both physically full and mentally comfortable with the person I wanted to become. Watching the restaurant patrons and others walking by, I felt like I had a range of styles and personas that made sense for me. Now, I just had to find a shop that would be able to work the transformation I had in mind. Finding the right place might require a bit of a walk, but the Martian air was still as sweet smelling as it had been this morning and I had a pocket full of m-creds that needed a new home.

The first several clothing vendors I approached had some items that looked nice, but even with the help of a sales person, nothing came together quite right. I almost walked by a strange shop, a table really, with nothing on it but two large reading pads and a sign that read, 'Boutique.' The woman, sitting by herself, returned my gaze with only mild interest. She was striking, dressed in a black tunic and long skirt, with high-heeled black shoes. With deeply tanned skin and straight black hair that was neatly trimmed at shoulder length, she was a picture of quiet sophistication. This was a woman who could help me.

"You don't look like my normal clientele." Her voice was lower and huskier than I'd expected.

"Is that a problem?" I asked, probably with more hostility than necessary.

"Not at all. I like a challenge."

"I need a new look and I think you can help me." I tried to retract the claws.

"Why me? There are plenty of shops around here."

I couldn't understand what I had done to perturb her, so I pressed on. "Instinct."

She looked me up and down and then twirled her finger at me. I obliged by turning around.

"You're too skinny, but I could make something work. What do you want here?"

"I need clothing." I was a dumbfounded at her question.

"No. That's why you are at my shop. Why are you in Puskar Stellar?"

"I'm looking for someone."

"Okay. Good. How long do you plan to be here?"

"I don't know. Depends on if I find her."

"Her?" She jumped on it. I immediately wished I could rescind my words. Somehow she had me off balance.

"It's personal."

"It matters. I need to know who I'm dressing," she insisted.

"I don't even know your name."

"Kathryne. Yours?"

"Lena."

"So, Lena. Who is this girl you are looking for? Does she owe you money?"

"No. Look, I don't even know if she's here. I just need to find her."

"A friend then. Is this friend in trouble?"

"What does this have to do with clothing?"

"Humor an old woman." She grabbed one of the reading pads and started swiping, no longer looking at me.

"I'm looking for my sister." I felt defeated.

"See. That wasn't so hard. Can you swing thirty-five hundred? She looked up from her reading pad."

"You don't even know what I want."

"No. *You* don't know what you want. You obviously are from off-world and have never shopped for clothing in your life. I, on the other hand, have been fitting women with clothing for most of mine. What do you think we've been talking about?"

"What? Are you always this difficult?"

"Yes. At least I answer your questions. How about it?"

"How about what?" I was fuming at this point.

"Don't be dense. Can you swing thirty-five hundred m-creds?"

I looked at her for several minutes, and she returned my stare, neither of us looking away. I finally made a decision. "Yes. I can swing it."

"Good decision. Come back in two hours. And while you are out, fix that hair. I won't have you wearing my clothes looking like that."

"Anything else?" I could feel the flush in my face.

"One more thing. Stop and see my friend Emir. Pay for and pick up two small devices. I need them for your clothing." Kathryne reached into the air just in front of her eyes and pinched her fingers. She held her hand toward me, as if to drop something at my feet. I held my reading pad forward and she released her fingers. Emir's Emporium showed up with an address.

I left Kathryne's company, relieved to be away from her. Emir's Emporium was several blocks away but in the direction of Punjay's Pawn. When I arrived, another dark-skinned man with thick hair met me at the door. I wondered if there was a settlement of a particular nationality here.

"You must be Lena," he said.

"Yes. Kathryne recommended you. Are you Emir?"

"I am indeed. She sent the specs for a couple pieces. I have them in the back."

I followed him past vac-suits, weapons, racks of blaster rifles, flechette pistols and all different types of weapons and armored clothing. On a back table he showed me two items. They were both small rectangular devices not much bigger than the end of my thumb.

"Power packs," Emir explained before I could ask. "Flexible, regenerating, parasitic, top of the line. Kathryne only works with the best." The packs didn't look like much, so they must be expensive if he was selling them this hard.

"Anything else?" Emir asked. "I have the biggest selection in town. You need it, I either have it or can get it.'"

"How about a small pistol?"

"Blaster or flechette?"

"I'm not sure. Needs to be small and if I have to use it I don't want them getting back up."

"Blaster then. Flechettes with stopping power are bigger. Personally, I like their control; your AI can adjust the flight while the dart is en-route. Nothing beats a blaster for putting 'em down, though. I know just the thing. Of course you know blasters aren't legal on Puskar Stellar and you will need to keep it locked up?"

"Of course."

Emir walked over to a shelf and moved a few boxes around. He finally found whatever he was looking for. He returned, opened a box and pulled out a small pistol. It was small, the barrel half again longer than if I simply pointed my finger. The grip fit easily into my hand. I hadn't realized that weapons were made with smaller grips for a woman's hand. I would definitely have picked out this gun if I'd only known what to ask for. It would be easy to hide.

"Perfect fit," Emir said. "Your thin fingers are a little unusual. Interest you in a blade? Nice looking girl like you can't be too careful. More subtle than a blaster, too."

I thought about it. I hadn't really considered myself a knife-type person, but his point about subtle was a good one. "I don't have a lot of places to hold a blade."

"I have just the thing. Top of the line. Only problem is the cops will take it if they find it on you." Emir disappeared into a back room and reemerged with a flat, black stick the length of my index finger. He handed it to me.

"Close your hand on it." I closed my hand around the flat stick and it puffed up, allowing me to grip it easily. The surface of the device felt like the handgrip of the blaster Emir had just shown me. It was comfortable and would be difficult to drop.

"Flick it away from your body, but don't drop it. You can't imagine how many people throw this the first time I show it to them."

I flicked my wrist away from my body, not sure what might occur. A small glowing line, the length of my hand, extended from the end of the device. Emir put an apple on the table.

"Sweep through it, but try not to hit my table," he said.

I did as he asked and when the apple moved only slightly, I felt just a small amount of pressure. Emir picked up the top of the apple and took a bite out of it. The blade had cut the apple neatly in half. I couldn't imagine what it would do to my arm if I missed. Emir must have suspected my concern.

"It won't cut you or your clothing. For that matter it won't cut someone you are touching. Give it a little harder flick, but do it away from everything."

I did as he bade and the blue light grew to nearly two-thirds of a meter. I was holding an extremely thin sword.

"Is this legal?"

"Not strictly speaking, so you should be careful." He handed two small squares to me. "Give these to Kathryne." He put the blaster pistol back in its box. "Remember. If these weapons don't work out for you, I have many more choices. Emir either has it or can get it. Swipe?" Emir gestured to his payment terminal. I saw the total of twenty-four hundred m-creds. It was going to be an expensive day.

My next stop was Ballance Electronics. I got help from a young woman and found a nice matte silver device that rested behind my ear and could telescope out in front of my eye to provide a HUD. The unit had a much higher quality display than my suit. I hoped it wouldn't cause as much eye strain. It was another six hundred m-creds, but I liked the way it fit. I could barely feel it on my ear, although I kept thinking something was brushing against my cheek as I walked. I would get used to it.

I still had an hour to kill and couldn't go back to Kathryne's without getting my hair fixed. She was right, it was in terrible shape. Some of the shine had started to return with regular nutrition, but it was still a mess with dry, split ends. I found a cluster of hair boutiques several blocks away and followed a pair of well dressed women into an upbeat shop. Several young men and women worked steadily on their clientele. The thin man who greeted me, was taller than me and dressed in tight fitting jeans and a loose black shirt.

"Are you here to make an appointment?" His smile was friendly but his message was clear, no open seats today.

"I'm in big trouble. I have a date tonight and I just arrived on Mars. I can't be seen like this." I caused my face to flush and willed tears to my eyes. Drama would be necessary.

"Oh, you poor dear, maybe we can squeeze you in. Let me check."

I reached out to him and gently touched his forearm. "You are so kind."

"As it turns out, I was just scheduled to go on break. Follow me. What did you say your name was? My name is Sam but they call me Sunny." I wondered if he would stop for a breath.

"Lena," I replied.

"Pretty name." He gave me a gentle push into a chair and spun it around, then ran his hands through my hair. "Lena, girl, you are a wreck. What have you done to your hair? Never mind, I don't want to know."

Sunny scrubbed, moisturized and trimmed my hair, then spun me around with a flourish. I hardly recognized myself in the mirror. My stringy, lifeless hair was full, like it had been when I was much younger. Sunny loved my silver-white color. He said it made me look mysterious. In the end, he did a fabulous job. I was surprised at how much I still wanted to feel pretty.

I tipped Sunny twice what he had charged and felt it was worth every m-credit I spent. I made my way back to Kathryne's with a bounce in my step.

"Oh, that's so much better," Kathryne said when she saw me. "You have such beautiful hair and you've treated it so badly. Promise me you'll not do that to yourself again."

"Never again."

She led me through her shop and stopped at a door to a small room. There were clothes draped over the back of a beautiful wooden chair. My eyes were drawn to long black boots leaning against the chair.

"Try it all on and we can see about a final fitting, though I doubt that will be necessary. Now that I see you again, you really are that thin. Boots go on last."

The clothing pieces Kathryne had assembled weren't significantly different than what she was wearing. A black skirt made of a luxurious, satiny material, clung to my body, making it only halfway down my thighs. On top, she had a long-sleeve beige shirt with a deep cut v-neck for me to wear. The black boots pulled up over my knees and held tightly to my legs, leaving a small amount of skin showing between the top of the boots and the bottom of the skirt.

I stepped out of the changing room and turned around at Kathryne's prompting.

"Beautiful. The fit is perfect. Now watch this." Kathryne tugged the skirt's hem and instead of pulling the entire skirt down, it simply extended. She let go, with the skirt just above my knees, and looked at me. I nodded my understanding. She pulled again and extended the skirt to my ankles. It was a beautiful look, but not particularly practical for walking.

"Not done." She ran a finger down the side of my leg starting at just above my knee and the skirt split.

"That's incredible, and the material feels great!"

"There's one more piece." She pulled a cloak off of a chair next to her and threw it over my shoulders. The cloak hung down to my ankles and had openings for my arms.

"Did you bring the generators from Emir?"

I handed her the two wafer thin squares.

"Perfect." She slipped them into a seam. "The cloak is active armor. Not only will it absorb small blaster fire, but most blades won't be able to penetrate it. No idea if you'll need it, but you look to have had a tough run of things. You can extend and shorten the cloak also. Styling is all mine, but you can set the length."

"It is all perfect. I don't know how to thank you."

"Swipe here, dear. You were smart to be truthful with me. I had intended to turn you away. You smell of trouble, but now I must know when you find your sister."

GONE TO GROUND

Back on the ship, I packed my vac-suit into one of the cases I'd taken from the Red Houzi hideout. A good chunk of my money had gone to clothing and I needed to be more frugal. The chests held at least four times the value of the platinum and coins, but that's where the money ended. I had to take good care of these, as there wouldn't be any more access to pirate loot.

Secure storage facilities in a major trading hub are apparently as common as horny men in a bar. The problem was, how safe were they? The facilities, not the men. I desperately needed to get these cases off the ship just in case the Red Houzi showed up sooner, rather than later. In the end, I chose two separate storage facilities. They both advertised the ability to pick up within the next two hours for a substantial up-charge. A representative of the local stevedore's union was required to be present while robotic carriers zipped up the ship's ramp, picked up the cases and trundled off.

I must have lost track of time, because I was startled when Benny pinged me. He was standing just outside the airlock.

"Hi Benny. What's up?"

"Want to let me in, Doll?"

"Be right there." I was pleased to see that the little troll had dressed up. I arranged the skirt so that it fell only halfway down my thighs and pulled a deeper V into the shirt. I lifted the cloak up so its length matched the hem of my skirt.

Benny was not only sporting a new, brightly colored blue shirt with large lapels, but he also appeared to have found a new pair of pants and dress suspenders. I might have made fun of him for the loud shirt, but I couldn't. He was making such an effort.

I opened the door and allowed Benny to get a look at me. I

could have worked it a little harder, but I was pretty sure I had him either way at this point.

"Aren't you just darling?" I asked, causing Benny to blush. "Where are we headed tonight?"

"K-Paul's Cajun. Feu Follet is playing."

Darkness had fallen while I was on the ship. I wasn't used to thinking about such things and I noticed the air had cooled considerably. A vac-suit kept my body at a consistent temperature, and now, without it, I had skin exposed. The discomfort wasn't critical, so I put my arm in Benny's and we walked together out of the ship lot.

K-Paul's was several blocks away and I was surprised at how the streets had transformed from a bustling marketplace to well-lit walkways. Light flooded out of the building through giant arched glass windows. Black-shirted servers worked around tables with red checked tablecloths. The music pouring out of the front door was loud.

"Had to bribe a guy I know to get a reservation. It's all about who you know," Benny said. He had to speak up to be heard over the noise. His raspy voice was having difficulty keeping up.

We received a few looks from the patrons. I wasn't exactly date material for Benny, if anything I was over-dressed. I exaggerated the swing in my hips. No better way to be forgotten than to act like an escort.

There was a raised stage in the middle of the room where the band played. A wisp of a man was holding an accordion and singing. I couldn't make out a word, other than it was loud. The rest of the band played stringed instruments and harmonized with the lead.

"Good, no?" Benny all but yelled at me. I nodded and smiled, not wanting to yell back. The waiter sat us next to a window, giving us a nice view of the street. It would be difficult to be in a bad mood at K-Paul's.

Benny ordered for the two of us. I had no idea what to order in a Cajun restaurant. When the food came out, it smelled delicious. Jambalaya.

While I was trying to work my way around the spicy food, my eye caught sight of something that caused me to break into a cold sweat. Alexander Boyarov. He was leaning against a building directly across from K-Paul's, staring directly at me. When we made eye contact, he gave me a knowing smile. Panic coursed through my body. I had to run. I started to get up.

Benny reached out his hand to grab me. "What's up, doll?"

I shucked off his hand, but sat back down. I reached into my coat pocket and pulled out my small hand blaster and pointed it at Benny under the table. He saw the gun and his eyes grew wide.

"Who did you tell?" I asked through gritted teeth.

"What are you talking about doll? Put the toy away." His raspy voice now sounded greasy instead of cute.

"You called someone. Reported my ship. Who was it?"

"Wasn't me. I was going to but we were getting along so well."

"Red Houzi, you stupid shit. Standing right outside looking at us. Was that the plan? Get me out of the ship and turn me over?"

"No doll, you got it all wrong." Benny stared at me imploringly. It was his mistake.

"So you already know he's there? I tell you Red Houzi is standing outside and you don't even look?" I was pissed now.

"Where? I don't see anyone." Benny looked out the window, but refused to look in Alexander's direction. No doubt he had been warned about giving Boyarov's position away.

"Benny. If you ever want to see me again you have to level with me. How many are there? He's here to kill me."

Benny looked away from me to the floor. "At least three. I'm supposed to get you out the back door. I didn't have a choice. I'd already called them before we started getting along. Can I help?"

"Will you help me?" I asked.

"What do you want me to do?"

We both stood and walked toward the back. Benny pulled out a small blaster that fit neatly into his oversized hand. He walked close to me and I could feel the barrel in my ribs.

When we got close to the back door, I pulled my nano-blade from the top of my boot and gave it a quick flick. I saw the blue glow of its extended blade out of the corner of my eye. I tore away from Benny and jammed the blade into his shoulder.

"You frakking bitch!" he bellowed. My heart was already hammering and my legs churned in panic, putting distance between us.

I made a mad dash toward the front of the restaurant. Two men at the back were odds I had no interest in. I ran into a waitress who was carrying a large tray of steaming food, causing the tray to crash into a nearby table. To her credit, she followed it down, trying to minimize the damage.

I heard blaster fire and saw charged rounds flying just over my head.

The restaurant erupted in chaos. Suddenly, I wasn't the only one running for my life. More shots sizzled past, sticking into the opposite wall. People are crazy dangerous when exposed to gun fire. I was thrown from my feet by a man barreling toward the door and I crawled under a nearby table.

I yanked the hood of my cloak over my head and the coat sleeves down to my wrist. I pulled the cloak's hem down the best I could, considering my position under the table. I rolled back out from under the table and looked for a group as close as possible to my own age and ran after them.

We didn't stop running until we were a few blocks away. I angled away from the group and darted into the shadows of a building. I scanned back and forth, trying to see if I'd been followed. There were too many people behaving erratically, so I really had no idea.

I straightened up and walked down the street, working very hard to keep my pace down and appear deliberate. Three sailors, who were obviously on leave, were walking in the direction I wanted to go. I waved and called out. They looked over at me and the tallest one waved back. I jogged over to them.

They were clearly drunk. The tall one took a look at me and was about to say something when I grabbed him by the crotch and gave him the kiss of his life. His breath was bad, but I'd experienced much worse.

"Whoa there, sister," he said.

I let go of his crotch which by now, communicated his obvious interest.

"You boys looking for a party?" I asked.

They exchanged looks and the tall one smiled widely. "Heck yah! I knew Puskar was gonna be a good layover! Get it … Layover!"

The three laughed loudly. Merry partygoers would not be on Red Houzi radar. I wrapped my arms around two of them and we sauntered down the street like we were lifelong buddies. They were a little handsy, but in fairness, I had started it.

Several blocks away, the crowd had thinned out and I was able to get a good view of the streets. No one was following. I felt a little sad for the boys. I had promised something I would never be willing to deliver.

"Okay boys. I have a confession to make." I stopped the group.

The tall one, Jerry, looked at me with genuine fear on his face. "You aren't a guy are you?"

I smiled at his horror. Of all the things in the world he had to be afraid of, being kissed by another guy was at the top of his list. I wanted to smack him. He'd had his hands on a good portion of my body and should have no questions as to my gender.

"No Jerry. I'm not a guy. But I wasn't totally honest with you either. I'm not a pro and I'm not going back to your room with you."

"What? Why?" Jerry whined a little.

"I needed your protection back there. My old boyfriend won't leave me alone and I needed to get out of there."

"What? Let's go back and get him!" Jerry was pretty volatile. I wondered how much he'd been drinking.

"No, we aren't going to go beat him up." I grabbed Jerry's hand. "Look, you guys are awesome, I'm really sorry about lying to you, but I needed out of there real bad."

One of the other two sailors stepped forward. "Well I'm not okay with it. You need to put out. You can't go promising that and then just leave us hanging. It ain't right." He advanced toward me and I dropped Jerry's hand and stepped back, pulling my blaster from under my cloak.

"Don't ruin it sailor. You did a good thing." I backpedaled further.

Jerry put a big paw on his buddy's shoulder, causing him to spin around angrily.

"Don't be a dick, Trey. Girl here was just trying to get safe, nothing wrong with that. She isn't a pro and we aren't doing anything she doesn't want." Jerry looked over to me. "Don't even know your name."

"Lena." I continued to back up.

Jerry pinched the air on his HUD and tossed it at me. His contact information showed up on mine. I grinned at him, turned and jogged off, putting my blaster back into the cloak.

Hail a taxi.

Moments later a small silver car descended to street level. I jumped into the leftmost seat and requested privacy mode. The glass darkened. I could see out but not as well as before. I knew from entertainment vids that the exterior glass was now obscured.

Show city map.

My HUD displayed a top view of the city. I was in the Open Air District on the far Eastern side of the city.

Show hotels within ten kilometers.

GIVE ME A WEEK

I awoke the next morning in a clean bed for the first time in as long as I could remember. The Martian sun flooded the small room with light through the open drapes. I was on the third floor of a hotel that was obviously meant for business travelers. The room had a large bed, a chair with a table, and a desk which doubled as a dresser built into one wall. It also had a private bathroom that was spotless.

I unwrapped a small bar of hand soap and grabbed the free bottle of shampoo and started the shower. I stayed in the steaming stream of water for half an hour until my mind switched to Jenny. I immediately felt guilty when I thought of all of the awful things that could have happened to her. I was enjoying myself and she could be sitting in a hellhole like the one I'd experienced at the hands of the Red Houzi.

Today I needed to make progress on finding her. Alexander might be looking for me, but I had given him the slip. I just hoped he had no way to track me. I turned the heat up in the room and sat at the desk, wrapped in a fluffy white towel with another wrapped around my head.

There were a couple of new messages from Alexander on my reading pad. I couldn't imagine him saying anything I would want to hear. It was possible he could slip in a clue, but I really didn't believe he had anything to do with Jenny. His goal was to upset me.

There was a message from Benny.

Heya Doll. I was hoping to see you at the hospital, or at least hear from you. They have me locked up in County Jail but they said they won't hold me much longer. I'm due in court in a few weeks for drunk and disorderly as well as illegal discharge of a firearm. I made bail and my lawyer says I might have to do a couple of weeks in jail, nothing big. I know it was a rotten thing to do - to turn you in to Red Houzi. You gotta believe me, I wouldn't have done it if I'd have known we were gonna be friends. Please give me another chance.

First off, I couldn't believe how gullible Benny really was. Second, I felt guilty for having played him so badly. He was locked up in jail and the only thing he was worried about was if he had ruined his chances with me. The thing is, I needed him and would have to keep using him. I did kind of like him, not like he wanted me to, of course. Someday I'd come clean with him and hope we could still be friends. Right now, I couldn't risk that he might not help me.

I took the towel off of my head and caused the reading tablet's camera to track my face, keeping my shoulders and face in the center of the frame. I sent a message back to Benny.

Benny, I'm so sorry I stabbed you. I know you are big and strong and can take it, but it must have hurt so badly. I was able to escape and have holed up where I don't think they can find me. I'll lay low for a while and hope they move on. They have probably already taken my ship, but that's okay. It really is theirs, I just needed to take it to escape. You need to be very careful with Alexander. If he thinks you and I are together he will hurt you.

I never told you why I'm on Puskar Stellar. My sister is missing. I think she might have come to Puskar on a ship called Domiva's Grace. Do you know anyone that can help me find her, or find information about Domiva's Grace?

I'm still so sorry for your arm.

I blew him a kiss and stopped the recording and sent it. Hopefully, he would have some ideas. I wouldn't leave it all to him, but I felt like Benny was probably a pretty resourceful guy.

I spent the next two hours searching information on ship arrivals and departures. Unfortunately, I finally figured out that most of that information is not publicly available. There were references to *Domiva's Grace* but nothing specific and certainly no schedule. They advertised passages to different destinations, but the information was nine months old.

I resolved to hire someone to help, but had no idea who might specialize in missing persons. There were plenty of advertisements for private investigators, but how could I tell who I could trust? I decided to reach out to Kathryne. For some reason, I didn't completely buy that she was just a clothier.

I switched from the reading pad to my earwig and was surprised when Kathryne answered my communication request. The background showed her sitting in her chair in front of her boutique.

"Yes?" I wasn't surprised at her terseness.

"Do you have a minute to talk?" I asked.

"I answered your call. Speak."

"I need a private investigator and was hoping you could help me."

"What made you think I could help?" Kathryne replied.

"I'm sorry, I must have been wrong. I won't bother you."

"Answer the question, child."

It took me a moment to figure out what question she was referring to. Everything was a test with her. I had to commit to the conversation before she would go any further.

"I think there is more to you than meets the eye." It was an over-step on my part but it also seemed that this was what she required.

"I see. You formed this opinion how?"

Frak, but I wanted to smack this woman. "It's just a feeling. I've had to learn to read people. I need help getting information about Jenny."

"Fair enough. I will help, but it will cost you. Be at my shop at five-thirty and send me what you know about your sister. Don't leave anything out."

I knew better than to ask about the cost. I would get as much from her as I could and pay whatever was necessary if it would lead me to Jenny. I sent her the small bits of information I had on Jenny and *Domiva's Grace*. It felt pretty slim but was all I had.

It was already late afternoon, so I caught the MAG-L (magnetic levitation train) back to a station within half a kilometer of Kathryne's boutique. There was a café fifty meters from her front door and it seemed like a good idea to see who might be entering her shop before our meeting. When five fifteen came, no one had moved into or out of the shop. I thought it seemed a poor way to run a business, but at least I wasn't walking into a trap.

The tables outside were empty and the front door was unlocked, although an old-fashioned sign that hung behind the transparent paneled door announced they were closed. I thought about knocking, but decided she was expecting me, so I pushed the door open and walked in. The lights in the shop were set low, which I took as an indication that she wasn't open for business.

I called out into the empty store, "Kathryne?"

"Back here, dear." She appeared in an open door at the back of the store. Something about her posture or tone set me on alert. I pulled the nano-blade from my boot. The handle expanded from its flattened form to fit perfectly into my hand.

Kathryne disappeared back into the room. Once I reached the door, I warily looked through. It was a smaller office with a wall of bookcases filled with large books and binders. Fabric samples were draped over and sandwiched messily between many of them. A single desk was shoved against the back wall and a small round table sat next to the door. Richly upholstered, wooden, straight-backed chairs were arranged around a table that might seat four or five people.

Kathryne stood next to a woman a few years older than myself, dressed entirely in black. Her pants were skin tight and showed off slim legs that disappeared into clunky, military styled, shiny black boots. She also wore a black jacket pulled tightly around her torso and made of the same material as her boots. Long black hair fell straight down her back. I couldn't see enough to tell where it ended.

She gave me the same appraising look.

"Natalia, this is Lena, the young woman I was telling you about. Lena, may I introduce my daughter, Natalia Liszt, private investigator." The dark haired woman stuck out her hand, compelled by the ritual of a formal introduction. I could see skepticism in her face.

"Call me Tali," she said. Her voice was a low alto like her mother's, but lacked the smoky quality.

I stuffed the nano-blade into a pocket of my cloak and accepted her hand. Her grip was firm, she was obviously strong, but didn't seek to crush my hand. Her face was passive, guarded. I supposed mine was the same. We were clearly not a very trusting bunch.

"Why don't you ladies have a seat? Lena, Natalia is one of the best investigators in Puskar. She agreed to hear your story because of an old woman's request. Natalia, play nice. I have things in the shop to clean up." With that Kathryne exited the room, leaving Tali and me to stare at each other.

"Well. That could have been more awkward," Tali said.

I chuckled and then asked. "Is it true? Are you a private investigator?"

"Yes, high end work mostly. I don't do divorce or worker's comp stuff. Kathryne tells me you're looking for your sister. The information she sent was pretty sparse. I found records on a Jennifer Dontal, from Terrence, with a deceased sister, Celina Dontal. I found a few other Jennifer Dontals, but none of them from the same age group. I presume this makes you Celina?"

"Yes. Did you find Jenny?" My heart was beating faster. Could it be this easy?

"Sort of. Which is not the answer you're looking for, I know. The thing is, I haven't decided to your case. Either way, I'll give you what I've found after we're done talking. That work for you?"

I was disappointed that she didn't have an easy answer for me. "Sure. That's more than fair." I couldn't afford to alienate someone with information about Jenny.

"You want to get out of here and get dinner? Do you have plans?"

She could have asked if I wanted to jump off a cliff and I would have agreed. "I'm starving." I lied, I still didn't get very hungry most of the time.

"I know this great little sushi bar in University Hills. Ever had sushi?"

"I have no idea."

"Well. They have different things. I just like the scene. It's right by the University, good energy. You game?"

"Absolutely." I said it with more confidence than I felt since Alexander was still looking for me.

"Ever been on a bike?" She asked.

"I don't think so. What's that?"

"Grav-bike. I've got an Indian, you'll like it. C'mon." She exited the room. "Mom, we're going to grab some dinner. I'll call tomorrow."

Kathryne was at the front of the shop. If she heard her daughter, she didn't acknowledge it. I followed Tali out the back door. Sitting in the alley was what I recognized as a motorcycle grav-bike. I hadn't originally put it together, since I'd only seen them in videos. The grav-bike looked similar to an old-earth motorcycle. The styling was such that everything had a swept back appearance. It didn't really look big enough for two people.

She threw her leg over the seat of the bike. There was a space no wider than five centimeters behind her. "Sit down tight behind me and wrap your arms around my waist. Try not to lean one way or the other, but hold tight. Closer is better. Don't worry, I won't bite."

In for a penny, in for a pound. This was about to get real personal, real quick. I slung my leg over the back of the bike and slid down behind her. The pitch of the seat forced my hips forward into her. I tried to lean back and put some distance between us.

"Sorry Lena, I know it's close, but lean forward. Otherwise you'll throw us off balance," she said.

I wasn't comfortable being close to another person yet, but this was different. She wasn't trying to get something from me. The warmth of her body made me realize I hadn't touched another person this personally without being forced or threatened, in a long time. I'd wondered if that part of me would ever be okay again. I relaxed and leaned into her, wrapping my arms around her waist and laying my head against her back.

"Put these on. Make sure you get your earwig inside, the wind can pull it out if you're not careful." She handed me a pair of wrap-around goggles. "We should probably wear helmets, but bikes are all about being free."

"Can you hear me?" Her voice came through my earwig.

"Yes."

"The goggles link us so we can talk. Don't take this the wrong way, but you smell nice."

I wasn't sure what the right way was, but I took it as a compliment. She smelled faintly of rosemary, I liked it.

"Whatever you do, don't let go. If we get into any trouble, try to stay as close to me as possible. We won't, but just in case. Ready?" She asked.

"Yes." I probably sounded hesitant to her but I wasn't sure what I was getting into.

The bike thrummed to life, subtle vibrations transmitted through the seat into my legs. The bike didn't make any noticeable noise but its power was intoxicating.

"Here we go." My stomach lurched as we launched forward. I pulled into Tali and closed my eyes hard. We were goners. The wind rushed by us at an alarming rate and it picked up her hair, which fluttered back on me. The goggles kept it out of my eyes, which was small comfort.

After a few moments we stopped accelerating, the wind was a constant battering force around our bodies. We were flying. It felt nothing like traveling in space. Wind, gravity and the constant push of the grav-bike beneath us, it was both terrifying and exhilarating.

"Any chance you could loosen up a little?" Tali asked.

I was chagrined to discover I had her in a bear-hug. It was a wonder she could breathe. "Oh, sorry." I relaxed my embrace.

"No worries. If you haven't been on a bike before, it's a lot to experience. You should try to open your eyes."

How could she possibly know my eyes were still closed? She

was right though, so I opened one eye in a squint. We were flying low at a couple hundred meters above ground level, not far above the tallest buildings. I opened my other eye and saw vehicles rushing past us. I loosened up a little more and looked to the other side.

"That's better. Pretty great, right? We're doing forty meters per second. Any faster and we'd get the attention of the local LEOs."

"LEOs?"

"Puskar Cops. They get grumpy if they have to chase me down."

"Oh. How far are we?"

"Few minutes, not far. You doing okay? Sorry about my hair. I should have tied it up. Look over to the left, that's downtown. We're over Coral Vista right now, just about to North Town. University Hills after that."

The tall buildings of downtown looked different from the back of a bike than when I was inside the cab. Silently we rode. I loved the feeling of the wind rushing by and the warmth of Tali's body. It was all so free spirited.

After fifteen minutes, Tali started descending. All of the nearby buildings had the same orange colored clay tile roofs. Some buildings were large, although none of them were over three stories tall. There were courtyards and paths all over the place. I guessed this was the University. Tali confirmed it.

"Puskar Stellar University. Good school. Completely free, just like all Universities on Mars. Only requirement is doing the work. If you can hack it, you can stay."

"I didn't know they were free."

"You have to be a resident, but yeah. Okay, here's our stop. She decelerated and landed in a parking structure."

"Aren't you worried someone will take it?" I asked as I handed her the goggles.

"Good luck with that. Security system goes ape-shit if someone other than me tries to move it." She smiled and put both sets of goggles into a pouch on the bike. She retrieved a couple of hair brushes and handed one to me. "It's better if we tie up the hair before getting on, but I love the feeling."

I accepted the brush and found I had some nasty tangles. I did the best I could and handed it back to her. She apparently had experience with detangling her hair, as her own looked like she had just taken a shower and brushed it out. Her fine black hair was longer than mine, reaching down past her shoulder blades.

"Okay, still good for sushi?" she asked.

I smiled back at her. To find Jenny I would have gone anywhere, but now having experienced the closeness and enjoyment of the bike ride, I'd be happy to eat whatever she wanted. "Only if I can buy," I answered.

"It's a deal."

The restaurant wasn't far from where we'd parked. The décor was minimalistic. A rusty colored stain had been applied directly over concrete and the tables were all high tops with tall stools. A college-aged girl seated us at a table overlooking the courtyard we had crossed to get here.

"Want me to order for you?"

"Just get me whatever you get. I'm not picky." It was an understatement. After a couple of years of near starvation, I was no longer off-put by unusual food. If it was clean, I'd eat it.

"Remember, if you don't like it, they also have some easy rice dishes."

"It'll be fine."

Tali ordered several items and asked for them to be served in the middle of the table. It was a nice way of letting me choose what I liked.

"Okay, let's get down to business. I need to know what I'm getting into. Tell me about Jennifer, how you guys became separated, and why you think she's on Puskar Stellar. Don't spare any details. The more I know, the more I will likely want to help."

"Can you? I don't want this to come out the wrong way, but how do I know you can help me?"

"Okay, got it. I can go first. I don't suppose Kathryne told you much about me, so I'll give you the short version. I joined the Marines when I was seventeen, just after I got my EMC

(Earth/Mars Citizen). I was accepted into special-forces shortly after that. Without getting into details, I left the service after ten years with an honorable discharge. I tried being a cop for a couple of years, but let's just say that didn't work for me. Twenty-six months ago I started a private investigation firm. I'm a solo act, but have lots of contacts. That's as succinct as I can get."

"You don't look … well, ok, that's impressive. I didn't mean to question you but I can't waste time. It's my sister."

"No. I agree. How could you know? And for the record, I age well. I'm thirty-one." She was right, she didn't look more than twenty-five from any distance. Close up I could see a hardness in the lines of her face which now made sense.

"That was me. Now, I need the scoop. Let's start with you not being dead." Her look wasn't unfriendly, but the camaraderie was at least momentarily lost.

"This is hard for me to talk about."

Tali reached across the table and put her hand on my arm. It was an intimate gesture and there was compassion in her eyes. "Don't give details yet, be brief. If it's important I will ask for more. Try to not to skip too much though."

I wanted so badly to trust her. In less than an hour, I'd become closer to her than any other person in the universe other than Jenny.

"Okay, here goes. On Terrence, both my parents died before I was twelve. By the time I was fourteen I was the sole provider for me and my sister. To start out with we had enough to get by. We spent virtually nothing. I dropped out of school to work more and keep us going. A mining colony is a terrible place to need money. The whole economy is about mining and if you're not a miner, you can't add value to the community. By the time I was sixteen, I turned to prostitution to help make ends meet. We weren't getting ahead, but Jenny was still in school. I don't think she knew what I did. One day I got invited to a party, there were supposed to be some big-shots there. I was abducted and taken to a Red Houzi base. Roll forward eighteen months. I escaped, made my way to Terrence and found out that Jenny disappeared, maybe to come here."

It was as dispassionate as I could make it, but the memories brought tears to my eyes. I refused to give into them. Tali didn't seem like the type to make decisions based on emotions and she needed to see that I was tough enough to see this through.

"That sucks. How did you get to Terrence and Puskar Stellar?" I found it odd to think that she simply accepted my story. Even as a summary it sounded pretty far-fetched.

"That's a long story all by itself. The clowns at the base where I was held, targeted a group that got pissed off and brought the fight to us. They basically kicked our asses. The captain was cool though. He told me that if I helped him, he'd get me out and he did. He even gave me the ship he captured on the base."

"Captain Liam Hoffen?" She asked.

"Yes. How did you know?"

"It's the sort of thing that gets around. So you were part of that mess. Where's your ship now?"

"Not my ship anymore. The place where I left it is crawling with Red Houzi. I think they're after me too."

"Why do you think that?"

"One of the pirates showed up in Puskar and tracked me down at a restaurant and then sent threatening messages."

"Seems like that might have been good information to share. Anything else?"

"Well, there's a guy from the place I landed the ship. Benny. He told Red Houzi where we were eating dinner and they came for us. The pirate that's after me is Alexander Boyarov. He's dangerous. But Benny's not a bad guy. They would have hurt him if he hadn't turned me in."

"Yeah, sounds like a real standup guy."

"He helped me escape." Was I so desperate for friends that I was willing to defend Benny?

"Okay, now tell me everything you know about your sister after you were abducted."

I sent Tali the correspondence I'd received from Jenny and also the conversation I had with Jenny's friend Misty regarding passage on *Domiva's Grace*.

The sushi arrived. I wasn't particularly hungry.

"Eat. It's not heavy and you can't let your body run down," Tali instructed.

I grabbed a few of the rolls from the nearest plate and nibbled on them as Tali reviewed the correspondence.

"Okay. Everything you say seems legit and I believe you. I'm not cheap. Seven hundred a day plus expenses. A week in advance. After a week we reassess. Sound fair?"

Neither of us realized just how much fair wouldn't cover what we were stepping into.

OH, THAT'S GONNA LEAVE A MARK

"I'll check in with you as needed this week," Tali said. "I mostly need to do some computer work. Expect a few hundred in expenses. I'll need to pay a nerd or two."

"Hah. Okay."

"Do you need a ride anywhere?" she asked.

"No, I'm good. Thanks for dinner, love this place." I said.

I watched her walk across the courtyard to the grav-bike. She walked gracefully, with no mind for just what those black pants did to college boys. I smiled as each boy along her path turned to catch a glimpse as she passed. It was hard for me to understand how someone that beautiful could also be Special Forces, but she didn't seem to be the sort to make things up.

It was getting late and I didn't have a place to stay yet. I walked outside and sat under a tree to do a search for lodging – maybe something that rented by the week. I wanted to see about the cases I had in storage. If the search took longer than a couple of weeks I would run out of money pretty quickly. My big concern was Alexander somehow tracking the cases and intercepting me when I got to them.

I found a furnished dive that rented week-to-week for two hundred a week. It was just outside the Open Air District in an area known as The Skeg. From this location it would be handy to get to where the cases were stored. As the cab approached my destination, I noticed that contrary to the other parts of town, this area was pretty sketchy. The buildings weren't particularly well maintained and some were crumbling. Given the wealth of the rest of the town, it was surprising a place like this would exist. But, I'd already paid for a week and I had a weapon.

The front of the building was in bad shape. At two hundred a week I had expected better. I should have left, but didn't have money to burn. It took the building super ten minutes to show up and grant me access to the building.

"Three-E. Make sure you're out by the end of a week. Anything left in the apartment is mine if you don't renew." The little man was dressed in a worn shirt and black jeans. He liked his position of authority and probably made a small amount of money selling the possessions of the inhabitants who had the bad fortune to forget his rule. As it was, I owned nothing that I wasn't already carrying.

The inside of the apartment wasn't as bad as the outside of the building had led me to believe. It was spartan, but clean. They probably had a cleaning bot to keep the units looking nice between visits. I noticed with a certain glumness that the shower didn't come with free shampoo, soap or a towel. I'd need to pick up those things, but not until tomorrow. I was beat.

Sometime in the middle of the night I felt a crushing pressure on my chest. I opened my eyes, still full of sleep. A big hand slapped me hard on the side of my face, just missing my ear, for which I was thankful. The pain brought me fully awake. On top of me was Alexander Boyarov, his knee pressed into my chest.

"Heya, crap for brains. Think I wouldn't be able to find you?"

I tried to push my way out from under him, struggling as hard as I could. I managed to slide to the side, out from under his knee, but he was too strong and wrestled me back down.

"Oh, you want a little fight?" He brought a big fist down on my face again and my head exploded in pain. I might have blacked out for a moment. When I came to again, Alexander was standing next to Olav Peetre, who had my gun leveled on me.

"Okay, little chicken. You ran away, but it is time to come back. I like what you've done with yourself. You were getting a little ratty back on the base.

I pushed myself up to a half sitting position, feigning more grogginess than I felt.

"How?" I asked.

"We are everywhere. You can't hide from me."

"Why?"

"Well, they put me in charge. I own the Baru Manush franchise now, I was just getting ready to head back there and need to take all of my stuff with me. That's what you are, Dontal. You're my stuff. Get it?"

I turned to Olav. "Olav, really? I spared you guys and this is the repayment I get? I could have spaced you - should have spaced you."

I was waiting for it. No way would Alexander allow me to try to turn Olav. Alexander was also predictable in his favorite method of punishment. Straight to the head. Once again, my head exploded in pain, but I kept my wits about me and on the way down I fished the nano-blade out from the top of my boot.

"Stop. You've made your point. I'll come with you, just stop hitting me." I really meant the last part. My face was bleeding badly and I didn't think I could take another hit like the last one and remain conscious.

"See Olav. You just gotta train 'em. Okay, Dontal, get up. You've caused me a lot of trouble so we ain't done here. Maybe if you go to the ship quietly I can be a little forgiving, although I wouldn't give me any more excuses."

I stood up slowly. It wasn't hard to pretend to be in pain. My head throbbed from the pounding I had taken. I flicked my wrist hard and caused the blade to extend fully and swung it around, catching Alexander's cheek and part of his chest. I had to give it to him, though. He was quick and jumped back, avoiding a much deeper, likely fatal cut. The wound on his cheek was deep, probably because as he pulled back his head dipped forward.

"Drop it, Celina," Olav said.

I didn't stop moving. Olav fired and missed me. My blade didn't miss his outstretched arm, however, and I severed his hand from it. The gun and his hand both dropped to the ground. It would have been handy if the gun had come free. Olav screamed. I lunged at Alexander but held back from impaling him with my blade.

"You have thirty minutes to get that hand over to the hospital so they can reconnect it," I said. I actually had no idea how long he had, but I knew a clean cut like that could be repaired. I kept the blade even with Alexander.

"You. Make a tourniquet and stop the bleeding."

"You'll never get away with this. I got two guys downstairs. You leave without us, you're as good as dead."

"Do it!" I said.

Alexander ripped the case of a pillow into a long sheet and tied off Olav's arm.

"Now. Give him his hand and put the gun on the table. You make one move toward me and I slice you open."

Alexander was brutish as well as arrogant. What he wasn't, was dumb. I still had the drop on him but he just needed to buy some time. I'd already tipped my hand. I didn't want their blood on my hands. Well, let's be clear, I didn't want to kill anyone, a little blood I was okay with. He pried the gun from Olav's detached hand and held it out to me. I saw the deception right away. The nano-blade's one major weakness was it couldn't hurt someone you were in direct contact with.

"On the table, Alexander."

He just looked at me, assessing if he could reach me before I sliced. He must have figured he would lose because he placed the gun on the table.

"Back up a step." He complied. I picked up the blaster and fired a round into the couch I'd been sleeping in. Alexander flinched, clearly expecting that I was aiming at him. I just wanted to make sure it would fire and couldn't spare looking at it closely.

With the blaster in my hand, I retracted the nano-blade. I was in a better position of control. I could shoot them from a distance if need be.

"Weapons on the table. Remember, I know where you keep 'em," I said.

It took some convincing, but they finally coughed up a pistol each and three knives. I remembered Alexander's knife, he was pretty fond of it.

"Take off your clothing."

"What? No way," Alexander protested.

"All of it. Otherwise I shoot you where you stand. Five. Four."

Alexander must have decided I was serious. He peeled off his vac-suit and wasn't wearing a liner. What a slob.

"Now help Olav off with his."

I finally had a pile of clothing and guns on the table.

"Get in the bathroom. You show your head for twenty minutes and I will blow it off. I'm gonna sit out here for a while, just so you know."

With both of them in the bathroom, I pushed a chair in front of the door. It wouldn't hold them for long but I didn't need much time. I dropped their clothing into the garbage recycler at the end of the hallway. No self-respecting pirate hunts naked, so I figured I had bought myself a short period of time.

Exiting the building, I didn't see anyone standing outside. The two-guys-downstairs thing was a bluff. No one would bring four guys to take one girl back. Big frakking mistake. Oh ... my head hurt. I walked briskly down the street. I wasn't sure where I was going but until I figured out how they had found me, I was in trouble.

"Hey! You! Stop there!" Oh frak, he really had brought people with him. I took off at a run, then stole a glance over my shoulder, nearly causing myself to trip. Sure enough two guys were giving chase. FRAK!

Open comm with Tali Liszt, emergency priority.

"Lena. What's up with emergency priority?"

"They found me."

"Where are you?"

Constantly stream coordinates to Tali.

"I'm ten minutes out. Hunker down somewhere."

Blaster fire erupted around me and I pulled up my cloak, remembering it had some capacity to absorb blaster fire. I hoped that wasn't just a sales gimmick. I turned the corner and sprinted down a street with very little lighting. I hoped the guys following me were my worst problem. How was I going to make it for ten minutes?

I wasn't in good enough shape to keep running, but my pursuers weren't coming right away. I hoped they had headed back to find Alexander and Olav. I needed to put some distance between me and Boyarov.

Hail taxi service.

My AI replied, *Taxi service not available in this area for another six hours.*

Frak!

I was running past obviously condemned buildings. In many spots the walls had completely crumbled away. Tali had said to hunker down. I was running in the open. It was mostly dark out but any vehicle would have the ability to light me up. I dodged through an opening in a wall and placed my back against it. My chest heaved with exertion. I wanted to see if I was being followed. I peered around the wall and didn't immediately see anyone.

Project light amplified path.

Immediately I was able to see an outline of the floor of the building, making up for some of the details my eyes couldn't quite make out. Still out of breath, I scrambled over piles of crumbling brick and other stuff which wasn't quite as pleasant. I climbed a dilapidated staircase to the third floor. The exertion was nearly too much and caused my head to throb even more. I felt faint but I wouldn't give in.

I took up a position by a broken-out window, being careful not to fall through the floor but also staying out of sight from the street.

"Lena, you stopped moving. Are you okay?"

"Yes. I'm holed up in an old building. I haven't seen them …" A light caught my eye. There was a vehicle moving slowly down the street. It stopped directly beneath my floor.

"What's going on? You stopped talking." Tali's voice whispered into my ear.

"They're here. Somehow they found me. I'm dead."

"What do you mean they found you?"

"They just pulled up in a car."

"I'm three minutes out. Shoot at the car. Do anything to slow them down. Don't give up, I'm coming!"

"No. You can't. They'll kill you too. Please don't." I couldn't bear to have one more person hurt because of me. They would take her and make her a slave.

I actually heard her snort derisively over the comm. "That'll be the day. Do what I'm telling you. Shoot the car and if anyone comes in the room where you are, light 'em up."

I hated that she was coming, but there wasn't much I could do at this point. I looked out the window again and they were already out of the car looking up at the building. I opened fire with two blasters. They immediately started firing back. I could see only two figures below firing up at me. I ducked back in to take cover. I moved to a different window and started firing again.

I felt a sharp pain in my hip, just below my waist. A round had been fired through my cloak. Whatever they had fired was a heavier round or my cloak was not able to absorb it. I'd been facing the window but the hit spun me around and I fell in a heap on the ground.

"Wow. The bitch never learns. You are such a pain in the ass, I should kill you right here and now. The only reason I'm not going to is because I want you to pay for what you've done to me. I'm gonna use you in the worst way." I could see Alexander's outline in the doorway.

Frak. How had they found me so easily and why didn't I just shoot him. Twice I had let him live and twice he'd hunted me down. If I ever had the chance …

"You make that up all by yourself?" Tali's voice asked from a dark corner of the room.

Alexander didn't hesitate but turned and fired in the direction of the voice. I also didn't hesitate. I had two blasters in my hands and fired them both repeatedly in his direction. He slumped to the ground.

"Hey. Maybe you stop that a minute?" Tali's voice came through my earwig.

It took me a moment to connect with the world around me and I finally stopped firing.

"Don't shoot, okay?" Tali's voice sounded like she was finding humor in the situation.

"Okay, I'm done," I replied.

I caught movement from the other side of the room, opposite where Tali's voice had come from and the direction Alexander had fired.

"How did you get over there?" The world darkened around me and I slipped from consciousness.

RECOVERY

I woke up with a start, head throbbing, and a terrible ache in my side. Not my worst start to a day, but it had to be in the top ten. At first I believed I was back on the Red Houzi base, as that was where I had most often felt this way. I opened my eyes warily, ready to take action.

"Whoa there girl, you're safe." I couldn't make out the speaker's voice initially, then it hit me. Natalia.

"Tali? Where are we?"

"Safe, kiddo. You're in my home."

"We gotta get out of here, they're tracking me somehow. You're in danger."

"If I'm in so much danger, then why are you the one who is on my couch, bleeding all over everything?"

"You don't get it. They have me bugged." I tried to sit up. Tali was sitting on a low table in front of the couch. She pushed me gently back down.

"Call me the exterminator, and you're right, you had two bugs on you. Sub-dermal, pretty cheap, the kind they use in the slave trade. Right now they are making their way through the sewers. I wrapped them in peanut butter. Rats carried them off. And you, my friend, have been shot up and beaten."

"What about Alexander?"

"Who? The diatribe guy?"

It took me a moment to catch what she was implying. "Yes."

"Yeah, not sure, we had to get outta there pretty quickly. I got a medic friend of mine coming over. You took a pretty good beating tonight. What in the world were you doing in The Skeg?"

"Trying to lay low. I've been staying at a new place every night."

"I see where you're coming from, but that's not going to be the right answer. Lay back, Jordy will be here shortly. I patched you up, but you're still bleeding internally and I'd bet you have a concussion. Was it diatribe guy who smacked you around so much?"

"Yes. He's the one who followed me. They are Red Houzi. I need to get out of here. I can't draw you into this any further. You should have left me there."

"Look. The only smart thing you did all night was call me when the shit got real. We'll deal with Red Houzi if it comes to that."

"Anyone home?" A male voice came from a room or two away. I had no idea of the layout of Tali's home. All I could see was Tali sitting on the table in front of me and an old brick wall behind her.

"Back here, Jordy."

Jordy was much closer to my idea of what a Special Forces operative would look like. Two meters if he was a centimeter, broad shoulders, tanned face, thick-muscular arms and a quick smile. He carried a small synth-leather case.

"Whoa, that's not right," he said, looking at me. If I didn't hurt so much I might have been offended. "Somebody's been using pretty girls for punching bags again. Want to tell me where he's at?"

"You take care of him for us?" Tali asked, her voice suddenly taking on a silky quality. Hmm, she had some game in that rock hard face of hers.

"Better believe it."

"Patch up Lena here first?"

"Wouldn't have it any other way. What hurts the most?" He looked at me with those crystal clear blue eyes.

"My hip."

"Alright. Let's take a look at it."

I started to peel my skirt downward, it was hard to shimmy it off while lying down. The material had lost its flexibility and there was a hole the size of my fist on the right side. I hoped my panties would maintain enough integrity to not also pull off. Fortunately,

Tali was quick with a blanket to keep as much of my dignity intact as possible. I appreciated the gesture.

"Ooh, that's a right nasty hit there. AK blaster round if I know my wounds, which I do. Bet that hurts plenty. Not a bad spot to get hit, though. Your skirt's a goner, and I wouldn't make any quick moves in those panties. Sure a shame about …"

Tali, who had been leaning over to also inspect the wound, drew back and slugged him in the shoulder. "You don't talk about a woman's panties."

Jordy's voice got a little higher, "I'm just saying … they aren't being held on by much."

She slugged him again.

"Okay I give! So you want the good news or the bad?" He looked at me, his bright blue eyes twinkling.

"Bad news." It hurt to talk.

"You're going to end up with a scar. It'll be a lot smaller than it is now, but no way are you getting outta this without a scar. I got the bleeding stopped and I'll put a patch on there that will get you up and running in a couple of days."

"I can't stay here." I said.

"We'll talk about that later. Let him finish," Tali said.

"Let's take a look at that pretty face of yours." Jordy gently held my face in his large hands. He probed my jaw delicately with his rough fingers. I jerked back when he touched my cheek. Jordy swore under his breath and for a moment I saw a shift in his face from the carefree playboy character to someone much more dangerous. He probed the rest of my face, carefully avoiding that spot. His finger paused on the long scar that ran across my right eye. "Story behind that one, I'll bet."

He waved a small instrument over my cheek and sighed with relief. "Oh thank you, Jupiter, it's just a fracture. So any other clothing you want to take off for me before I patch you up?"

He was laying it on pretty thick and I wasn't probably his best audience. He was exceptionally cute, but was also a player. I'll admit it was nice to have the attention of such a good looking man, but I was sure Jordy and I were never going to happen.

"No, you've seen it all." I didn't have the energy to banter with him.

His hands were steady and he took great care in applying medical glue to my battered face. He tsked at the sight of several other poorly healed lacerations on my face and gently applied a medical patch over my fractured cheek.

"Not even a whimper. This isn't your first time around the block. I'm sorry for being such a cad."

He turned to Tali. "You really going to give me his address so I can take care of him? Where's Godzilla?"

I saw Tali's face betray a smirk before she responded. "Godzilla's locked up in the bedroom."

"Thank God. That thing hates me." He turned back to me "Lena, it was lovely meeting you. Let me buy you some lunch when you're feeling better, sound good? And don't worry about this guy. I'm guessing you won't hear from him anymore."

A smile tried to break out on my face but it hurt so much I quickly quashed it. "Thank you Jordy."

"What's a guy to do if he can't rescue a damsel in distress?"

If I didn't hurt so badly I would have laughed.

"You want help with the creep?" Tali asked.

"Seriously? You really know how to hurt a guy. I'll go take care of him and you take care of the patient."

Jordy had given me some sort of injection and the pain subsided but I was also having a difficult time maintaining consciousness. I could hear them whispering a couple of meters away but I wasn't able to make out what they were saying.

When I woke up again, I was in a bright room, sun streaming through the windows. My face hurt but I no longer felt any pain in my hip. I also noticed I was wearing a thin white night gown. Most importantly, I had to use the facilities in the worst way.

I pushed myself up to a seated position and then froze in place. At the end of the bed lay what had to be a cat, only this one had to weigh at least twenty kilos. The giant orange tabby cat looked at me lazily and then resumed cleaning its fur.

"Oh, good, you're up." Tali walked through an open door into the room carrying a tray. "And you've met Godzilla. She doesn't normally take to people right away, but she seems to like you."

"I really need to go." I said.

"Look, we can talk about that later. You need to recover first."

"No. I mean, I gotta go."

"Oh. Ohhh! Don't worry about Godzilla, she's mostly harmless. Bathroom's at the end of the hall."

I scooted out of the bed, although I hated to leave its warmth. I was on the upper floor of a two story house. A railing separated a hallway from a staircase that led downstairs at the opposite end, just in front of the bathroom. I noticed ruefully that I was wearing a different pair of panties.

I looked at my face in the mirror and pulled back the med-patch. The healing had already started and the skin under my eyes had a greenish tinge. I'd completely missed the black and blue phase. Nothing looked too out of place other than some swelling, so I replaced the patch. I lifted the nightgown and pulled back the patch on my hip. All in all I had fared pretty well. Four on one and I was up and walking around the next day. Oh geez, I hoped it was only the next day.

I padded back to the bedroom where I found Godzilla spread out on her back receiving a rough scrubbing from Tali's fingers. The cat was making deep rumbling sounds that I was glad she hadn't made when we were alone.

"Hungry?"

I looked at the tray. Fruit, toast, and yogurt. It looked delicious, but I had to get this cleared up and get out of here. Tali was in danger. I sat on the edge of the bed.

"I shouldn't have called you and you shouldn't have come for me. I need to leave. You're in danger."

"Right. Let's have this conversation now," Tali said and stood up to face me. Godzilla rolled around trying to get her attention.

"These people, they'll never stop looking for me. They own me. I appreciate you saving me, but you don't know what they'll do to you ...," I said and then in a quieter voice, "what they've already done to me."

Tali's face contorted indignantly. "Own you?"

"You know what I'm saying." Tears of shame streamed down my face.

"No ... I don't." Tali sat next to me and pulled me close to her, stroking my hair. I sobbed. I remembered holding Jenny like this when we were scared.

"Let them come," Tali said with resolve.

"It's too much ..." I didn't know how to communicate this to her.

"Get over it. Do you know why Jordy came over?"

I shrugged. I wasn't sure.

"Because we were teammates. I've trusted that man with my life and I've walked through fire for him. He would never turn his back on me, nor would I turn my back on him. It's called honor, Lena. That's why I chose you."

"Chose me?" I had no idea what she was talking about.

"Yes, Lena. Honor. I'm an investigator. When I asked about your past, I was trying to learn about your integrity. I already knew everything you told me when we first met, but you didn't lie or embellish to make yourself look better. You gave it to me straight. No normal investigator would take your case once they learned about your past. You showed mercy to the very man who abducted you and twice you refused to kill the man who savaged you."

"You make it sound like I had so many options."

"That's the thing, Lena. You've had no end of options but you choose personal sacrifice every time. Get this straight though, no one owns you. You hear me?"

"I know."

"This wasn't your fault. You didn't ask for this, bad people do bad things. It's horrible, but it's true. You were doing the best you could for your sister and they took that from you. You are not less of a person for doing that, you are more. The only thing you have to learn is to stop hating yourself."

I wanted to believe her but I wasn't prepared to deal with it. "What now?"

"Good. Now, you eat. You've been down for three days."

"Three days? I thought Jordy said I was all fixed up?"

"He lied."

"What a coward."

"Couldn't agree more. You feel up for a trip?"

"Where we going?"

"One of my nerds says she has something, wants me to come take a look."

"Is this about Jenny?"

"Yes."

"Let's go!" I stood up.

"How about some clothing?" Tali asked.

I looked down at the thin white nightgown and laughed, despite myself.

"Mom will be crushed. I haven't had the heart to tell her your skirt got ruined. That was an expensive piece. Mom is pretty high-end. You'll have to settle for leathers. You're smaller than I am but I have some stuff I can't wear anymore."

I wanted to ask how I had gotten into the nightgown or even flown back to her house. Surely she hadn't tossed me on the back of her bike. I figured it would come up at some point.

"Sounds good, think my boots will go over them?"

"Probably not, but don't worry, shoes I have in abundance."

I followed Tali into another room on the second floor. It had been converted from a bedroom to a dressing room. One entire wall was covered with shelves filled with shoes and boots of every kind. Tali immediately started rummaging through a stack of folded clothing. She handed a pair of white synth-leather pants to me.

"Try those. I have a pretty good eye for size. Lots of weekends working for Kathryne."

I pulled the pants up underneath the nightgown. I had to wiggle to get them over my rear.

"Show me already!"

I lifted the nightgown and did a little twirl. I loved how the leather felt on my skin.

"Oh, they never looked that good on me. Merde, Jupiter sends me a model to test my humility. I've got these boots ..."

By the time I got out of her dressing room the only thing I had left of my own was my cloak. If it hadn't had an active armor component she would have replaced it too. I felt reassured to have my blaster back.

The house must have been a couple of hundred years old. The stairs creaked as we went down and the walls were uneven. Tali assured me that the bones of the house were solid, but the original building supplies were all manufactured from materials readily available on Mars surface when Puskar Stellar was first built.

When we left the house, I realized we weren't in town. I saw nothing for kilometers other than the shed Tali led me to.

"The wind gets pretty bad out here. If I don't park the bike in the shed it gets messed up."

"Is all this yours?" I asked. It seemed incredible to think someone could own this much land.

"Yup. It's an original homestead. Plenty of room for Godzilla to run around."

Taking off on the grav-bike was considerably more exhilarating with my eyes open this time. Puskar Stellar's skyline was off in the distance. Tali continued to accelerate until we were moving at an incredible speed.

"How fast?" I felt like I had to yell. The bike's protective shield extended on the front but we were still being buffeted pretty soundly.

"A little over a hundred meters per second. We're coming in from the South. It's why I was able to get to you so quickly the other night, no traffic or LEOs out here."

Once we hit town, she slowed significantly, as there was traffic as well as speed limits. We didn't talk much as we flew over town. I recognized the orange tile roofs of the University about the same time Tali slowed even further and set us down on a parking ramp.

"Student?" I asked.

"Associate Professor. Goes by the name of Bit Coffman and she's a real character. Be best if we brought some snacks with us."

After picking up a large carbonated drink and a big bag of jalapeno flavored popcorn, we finally arrived at the side door of a small brick house with the same tile roof as the rest of the campus. Tali knocked on the door.

The woman who opened it was tall, just a little heavyset and had buzz-cut red-blonde hair. She filled the doorway with her large frame.

"Heya bitches." She looked at the large drink in my hand and the bag of popcorn. "That'd better be for me."

I handed her the drink and she smiled. "Come-on-in-and-bring-the-popcorn." She spoke almost too fast to follow and disappeared into the house. Tali was first through the door and I stayed close on her heels. Bit's home was a single room efficiency which probably hadn't seen a thorough cleaning since she'd taken residence. A table, in what I would have classified as the dining room, was loaded with electronic equipment and vid screens. Wires were strewn everywhere. I couldn't imagine what all of it was used for.

Bit dropped heavily into a plush chair and pulled it in close to the table. "Just set the popcorn down. I just had some salty and now I need some sweet."

Tali pulled a candy-bar out of a coat pocket and put it on the table next to her.

"Oh sweets, you really are the best. So, this girl you gave me. She's in with a bad crowd. You really got your work cut out for you here. Her sister's a dead whore and best I can tell, *Domiva's Grace* is running slaves. Not sure if she was a volunteer or not, sister like that 'n' all."

I winced at the reference but didn't say anything.

"Maybe put your sensitivity filter on there a little?" Tali said.

Bit spun in her chair and looked at me. "Oh, shite. Relative?"

I looked back at her and made a decision. "Dead prostitute."

"Oh, crap, no shite. Hey look, I'm sorry. I really didn't mean anything."

I stopped her. "How about you make it up to me and help me find her. I guarantee she isn't a volunteer."

"Really, I'm sorry. I just say whatever comes to the top of my head."

"What'd you find?" Tali asked.

"zeatch this." She spun back around and one of the vid screens showed a ship I presumed was *Domiva's Grace*. Jenny was talking to the call box, and carrying a small bag. She looked tiny standing there next to the ship. Bit fast forwarded a few minutes and a boy not a lot older than Jenny opened the door and escorted her in.

"That was two months ago, give or take, on Terrence. I've watched every bit of footage from that ship and she never got off. I tracked three different person-sized or bigger crates that were off-loaded and followed them to their destinations. I saw two of them opened and one is still sitting in storage."

"You watched that crate for two months?" I asked, not completely buying what she was selling.

"I don't watch every minute but I have a program that catches the highlights when stuff changes. Not very high tech, to be honest.

"How about after that?" Tali asked.

"The ship flew on to Delta. Nothing was offloaded, but they might have picked up another girl. Can't be completely sure, she didn't just walk up to the ship like the target."

"Jennifer," I said.

Bit turned to me with a chagrined look, her already fair skin turning bright red. "Right. Jennifer. Sorry. So after Delta they went on to Jeratorn. Lots of packages taken on and off. I have trackers on six of the offloaded ones now. They aren't drawing any interest. So that's it."

"That's it?" Tali and I asked at the same time

"Oh, wait, right. *Domiva's Grace* is en route to Puskar Stellar. They'll be here in a little less than a week, give or take." Bit took a long drink of fizzy soda.

"Standard fee?" Tali asked.

"Already sent you the bill. I also sent you a copy of the vids. Remember who loves you, Tali-whacker."

"No nicknames, Bit," Tali admonished.

DOMIVA'S GRACE

We left Bit's apartment and Tali was in the mood for pizza, so we stopped at another one of her favorite hangouts close to campus. I secretly wondered if she regretted skipping college when she joined the Marines.

"You just can't beat this." I watched in awe as she finished a fourth piece of the large pie in front of us. One slice and I was more than done, but not Tali. It was odd, she might outweigh me by fifteen kilos, but ate like she'd never be allowed to eat again.

"So I'm thinking I will have to get on that ship. Maybe I'll try to break in," I said.

"No good, too much security around those big freighters. They'll shoot first, ask questions later."

"Any ideas?" I asked.

"Hold on. I got an urgent comm coming in." I barely understood her since she had just taken another giant bite of pizza. "Repeat last." The change in her demeanor was immediate, something was up. "Okay. Thanks Bit, we owe you big."

I waited impatiently for her to finish. "Is that about Jenny?"

"Sort of, *Domiva's Grace* just landed. Bit's working on getting live video. She's better at post-mortem however. If we wait for night, we could tag along with some of the crew. They probably have shore leave. We should be able to get in the ship that way."

My heart raced. It wasn't a terrible idea, but there were too many ifs. How could we be sure they would get leave before they unloaded? It was then an idea hit me. "Let me make a call. I have an idea."

Tali looked at me questioningly.

"Give me a second," I said.

Open comm with Benny.

Benny's raspy voice answered, "Heya, Doll. I was hoping you'd call. What can I do ya for?"

"I need your help, Benny."

"Uh oh. You in some more trouble?"

"It's not me. I need to get on a ship that just landed."

"At my yard? We've been pretty quiet."

"No. It's a family freighter."

"Oh, that won't be easy. Tons of security around them."

"What about the people who load and unload? Can't they get past the security?"

"Stevedores. That's all union jobs. Mostly mechanical with some supervisors."

"Benny, it's important. Could you get us on as supervisors if you had some money?"

"How much money we talking about, Doll?"

"What would it take?"

"Might be as much as a couple thousand."

"Your cut in there?" I asked.

"Ah, you hurt me."

"Benny."

"Yeah. On the house this time. Let me make some calls."

I hung up with Benny. "I think I can get us both on. I know I shouldn't have spoken for you. You don't have to go, but I couldn't sound flakey to Benny."

"Maybe you haven't figured it out yet, Lena, but I'm on Team Lena now. In for the duration. Isn't Benny the one who sold you out to the Red Houzi?"

"It's complicated."

"You trust him?"

"On this I do."

"There's a uniform replicator over near Kathryne's Boutique. We can change at her shop."

"He hasn't even called back."

"He will."

I received the call from Benny while we were in flight to The Open Air District where Kathryne's Boutique was located.

"It's a go. You have half an hour to get to the yard. The boss will ping you. It's thirty-five hundred and I had to call in a few favors. Hope you have the funds."

"I owe you one Benny. You still interested in dinner?"

"Yeah, Doll. Maybe you pick the place this time."

"It's a date Benny, I promise. If I get through this thing, it'll be you and three of the best looking women you've ever seen, hanging on your every word."

"Ohhhh." Benny was speechless.

As promised, I received a comm from Bruno Bentrod before we even got to Kathryne's with our uniforms. I was surprised at just how brazen he was. The communication had a thirty-five hundred m-cred required payment attached. In exchange I had two identity patterns that we could replicate at any Class-1 replicator. I suppose they had to hire people all the time, but the whole thing seemed like it lacked any real security.

The stevedore uniform was a loose white coverall. The middle constricted with an integrated belt. It wasn't very flattering, but the outfit was inexpensive to replicate.

"I suppose they get disposed daily," Tali mused as we looked at each other. "They will be scanning for blasters, but they won't pick up your nano-blade if you put it in your boot."

We were a few minutes late, but I figured that was probably keeping with the role. Bruno wasn't impressed.

"Get over there and oversee the mechs. Check off every crate with the corresponding line on the pad. It's not transporter science but union agreement says we inspect every piece that gets unloaded. Now get a move on!"

Tali and I jogged to where *Domiva's Grace* was parked. I couldn't have walked if I wanted. Jenny had to be on that ship.

The freighter was a large blocky ship that sat on four giant circular thrusters. It was rectangular, twice as tall as it was wide, with rounded corners and a round nose on the top. A series of five doors were evident on each of the five levels of cargo bays. A lift was already in place, raised up and providing a wide platform even with the bottom of the lowest bay door. An elevator on the side of the large lift waited to take us up to the platform.

In front of the elevator, a young man sat on a chair, doing his best to look bored or annoyed. When he opened his mouth I could tell which he was going for. It was the boy from the video. He'd let Jenny onto *Domiva's Grace* on Terrence. It took all I had not to say something.

"You certainly took your sweet time. Been sitting here for the better part of an hour."

I nodded and moved to get on the elevator.

"Hey, wait a minute. I gotta scan your creds." He jumped up from his chair.

"Make it snappy. Maybe you could give us a little advance and you wouldn't be stuck sitting here," Tali said.

The kid harrumphed and accepted our freshly printed credentials. I held my breath, but he handed them back after a limited inspection.

"We're only unloading decks one through four. You aren't allowed on deck five. Got it?"

Tali replied, "Sure kid, whatever's on the list."

The elevator dropped us off on the platform and we walked past three large container-moving robots. The robots had an upright portion that was knee height and ten centimeters wide on one side. Two large forks, a meter and a half long and set apart by half a meter, were connected at nearly ground level to the upright portion. They were used to slide under the containers.

The cargo hold door wasn't open, so we looked at it for a few minutes. I was starting to wonder if we were missing something when the door slowly lifted out of the way. The hold was completely packed with containers all the way up to the top of the doors.

The robots came to life and fired their arc-jets. They jetted up and neatly slid their forks beneath three of the centermost containers. The middle bot pulled its load out first. I immediately understood why there were three of them. The container on the right side started to slide when the middle container began to move. The bot on the right side made adjustments until the middle container slid free.

With the container loose, the bot dropped to the platform faster than I was comfortable with and slid over next to me. I looked at the reading pad Bruno handed me and noticed a highlighted row with numbers that matched the container held by the robot. I touched a virtual button that read 'confirm' on the pad. The robot raced off the platform and dropped immediately out of sight.

"Where do they go?" I looked at Tali.

She shrugged. "I imagine they have a warehouse."

I felt a breeze next to me and Tali's eyes widened. A loaded robot had dropped down next to me, waiting for me to confirm its payload. I looked at the tablet which had a new number highlighted. I checked and the AI had once again identified the correct item. I hit the confirm button and it raced off after its buddy.

I knew what was coming next so I waited and, sure enough, the third robot dropped down with its package. I looked down and, of course, the correct number was highlighted.

"So … this isn't an extra challenging job then." I said.

Tali shook her head with a grin.

"Hey! You can't get started without us." Two men jumped off the elevator and angrily gestured at us.

The first robot returned and slid under another container, lifted it and returned to my side. I now understood why they moved faster than I liked. Once you knew what to expect, you might not want to wait around too long.

"Can't have it both ways, dickhead. You can't get your little gopher to whine at us for being late and then decide we're going too fast. Time is money. Get your shit together or do you want me to report abusive behavior?" Tali was several centimeters shorter than me but she wasn't intimidated by anyone.

"Stow it, Jep. They've moved three containers." The second man was older, maybe mid-thirties. They both had several days beard growth and I caught a whiff of body odor as they approached. I found it odd, considering most suit-liners could remove odor for many days. Ugh, unless they weren't actually wearing liners. In addition to their bad personal hygiene they both were sporting holsters with blasters.

Jep, the angry younger one, also held a pad. "Which ones you get already?"

I showed him my pad, "Try to keep up, we've got a break in thirty minutes."

"What?"

"Union rules."

"Crap. Okay, I got 'em."

"You sure?"

He just looked at me. I turned to the robot that was waiting patiently for me. I confirmed the number. Apparently he got the same on his and the robot took off. The whole process felt like it could be automated.

I wanted to discuss things with Tali. We needed a plan that would get me inside that ship so I could search for Jenny. As it was, we could only see a bunch of closed containers. They were so closely packed that she certainly wasn't in any of them.

Thirty minutes in, the first hold was half empty. "Smoke 'em if you got 'em," Tali announced.

I looked at her. "Smoke what?"

"Never mind. I need a coffee."

"Coffee? Now?" I asked.

Tali raised an eyebrow. "Yeah, remember we didn't get one on the way here."

I had no idea what she was talking about but I'd go along with her. "Oh, right, can't believe I forgot."

"You boys want to grab a couple of coffees for us?"

"Not likely." Jep was quick with an answer.

"Righto. Okay, hold our spots. We'll be back as soon as we find some coffee."

"Leave your tablet at least," Jep complained.

Tali was quick with her response. "Not likely." She mimicked his voice.

"Frak. Fine. I'll have the little turd get 'em if you get back to work."

"Coffee first, maybe we'll make it a whole hour if it's nice and hot."

The kid who had greeted us showed up with coffees. I tasted it. Bitter - big surprise.

"Well. Back to work then," I suggested.

We continued unloading until the first hold was empty.

"Jep, how about you raise the platform so we can get started on number two," Tali said.

"I thought you guys always did that."

"Nope. Drinking my coffee. More efficient breaks this way."

Jep shook his head like we were messing with him but raised the platform.

Ninety minutes later, Tali's plan became evident. We were halfway through the fourth cargo hold and it was clear Jenny wasn't there. The coffee had worked its way through my system and I needed a break in the worst way. Tali noticed my discomfort and nodded.

"Break time," I said.

"What now?" Jep had lost his patience. In his defense, we had been pushing his buttons for the better part of a couple of hours.

"I gotta tinkle," I said with my best girlie voice.

"OH MY GAWD!" Jep exhaled. "Fine. We'll wait. How about you?" He looked at Tali.

"Stuff it," she replied.

"Back in fifteen. You know you could let me use the head," I said.

"Not likely," Jep said.

The emergency was real. I took the elevator down and went to the Stevedore's Union office. Fortunately, Bruno wasn't around. I finished and got out of there, walking slowly back to the ship trying to formulate a plan. I just couldn't come up with anything.

"You sure took your time. Let's get this done." Jep had cooled off a bit.

"Bad news, boys," Tali said. "Guess I have to go after all."

"You've got to be kidding me. What kind of crap is this!? I'm going to report you freaks."

"Oh, I suppose we're done here then if you're just going to report us," Tali said.

"No. Wait," he said.

"Look, Jep. I'm sorry we got off on the wrong foot. But that little creep you had greet us needs to learn not to mess with the union and you boys have been getting the brunt of it. How about you let me use the head real quick and we'll wrap this up? Otherwise I'll be back in fifteen or twenty. It's a bit of a walk to the Stevedore's Union."

"I'll take her," the mostly silent older one offered. He hadn't said more than five words the entire time we'd been there.

"They're not supposed to be on the ship."

"It's not a problem. I think I can watch one little girl." His leer wasn't overt but I caught it.

"Fine. Let's get this done already," Jep complained.

Tali and the older guard walked over to a ladder leading to a ceiling hatch. She scrambled up in front of him, opened the hatch and slithered through. I walked over to the built-in ladder and watched them move through the ceiling.

I heard Tali say, "Geez, it stinks in here. You guys have some rotten food?"

The guard said something I didn't quite catch.

Jep and I waited in silence for better than five minutes.

"What's taking them so long?" He asked.

Tali's legs came through the ceiling as she lowered herself down the ladder.

"There they are," I said cheerfully. "Time to finish up." I picked up the tablet and walked over to the waiting robot.

Jep looked at Tali's descending figure and hesitated, but his impatience got the better of him. He followed me to check off the container.

Tali dropped him with a quick punch to the kidneys. He wasn't unconscious but he was in too much pain to do anything but fall to his knees.

"Shut the door," Tali instructed calmly.

I found the panel and depressed it. It didn't do anything.

"Probably need a crew member."

Tali pulled Jep to his feet by brutally twisting his arm up behind his back, bringing it up just under the back of his skull. She shoved him to the bay door and placed his hand on the panel. The door lowered, leaving us in the low light of the closed cargo hold.

"There are pens in the fifth hold," she said.

"Pens. Like animal pens?" Then it hit me. I sprinted for the ladder and climbed. I was breathing hard when I finally pulled up through the ceiling. I pulled the nano-blade out and extended it to full length. The stench was overwhelming, a smell I immediately recognized. I had lived in that stench, it was part of me. I felt sick.

I rushed around a wall of containers and saw the pens. There were more than twenty stacked along opposite sides of the hold. I counted eight girls. The youngest appeared to be less than ten. The bile rose in my throat and I wanted to hurt someone. I ran to the first pen and instinctively put my hand in. The girl reached for me. I tried to open the door, but the lock panel wasn't budging.

"Don't touch that!" Tali yelled from across the hold. I turned and saw Jep stumble before her.

I moved between the pens, saying Jenny's name to each of the inhabitants. I already knew she wasn't here. I had gotten a good enough look at them.

"Take cover!" Tali exclaimed.

I spun around to blaster fire. Tali had positioned herself behind Jep and was dragging him backwards. She was firing at the small corridor between the stacks of containers that separated the back of the hold and the section we were in with the girls.

"Open the door!"

"Here. Cover me!" She threw a blaster to me. It slid along the floor, not far from my reach. I scooped it up and fired randomly at the containers.

Return fire lanced in my direction. It wasn't well aimed, but I could die just the same. I dove to the ground and crawled behind a crate. Blaster fire blew the crate apart and I felt something enter my shoulder. It spurred me on and I ran for new cover. I refused to go in the direction of the girls in the pens. I fired wildly, still not finding a good target.

The hold door started rising and made it a meter before stopping.

"All the way, Tali!" I yelled.

"It stopped. Someone is overriding it."

Open urgent comm Bit Coffman.

"Bit, help. We need you now!"

Bit's high voice came over, "Who is this?"

"I'm with Tali. We met two days ago. Can you forward my vid recording?"

"Who? Sure, no problem."

"Do it now! We're being fired on. Forward it to the police. They have slaves on board!"

"Oh crap! Okay. Wait. Don't make me nervous."

I looked around so that I captured the girls in the pens. The door of the hold started lowering.

"Get out, Lena!" Tali yelled. "It's closing!"

"Not without them."

The gunfire stopped.

"Where'd they go?"

The hold door closed completely.

"They have us trapped," Tali explained. "They're going to space us all. You should have gotten out."

"Right. How about you, Jep? They going to space you too?"

Jep was holding his arm gingerly. I suspected Tali had dislocated it, given the angle it was hanging. "Frak you! I knew there was something off about you."

"Look, dumbass, we're all going to die in twenty minutes if we don't come up with something. If you don't think they'll space you, you're crazy."

He thought about that for a moment. "You've killed us all. You crazy assholes!"

"Any escape pods on the cargo levels?" Tali asked.

"For cargo? No." Jep was sullen.

"Try the door again. They can't take off with an open door."

Jep tried the panel but it flashed red.

"Open the cages then. We need to get the girls out." I said

"Focus on something useful," Jep retorted.

I leveled my blaster at him. "That's your one chance. Open the cages or I'll waste you."

Jep grumbled and opened them. The ship vibrated as the engines fired up.

"Try the hatch. See if we can get out."

The ship started lifting and Tali scrambled up the ladder. She tried the hatch but it was closed tight. I looked back, the girls were huddled together. I wasn't sure if we had saved them from a worse fate. I very well could have killed us all. They deserved better. I had failed them.

Tali slid down and grabbed the blaster from me. At first I thought she was going to shoot Jep out of frustration, but she was more focused than that. She took aim on the panel next to the hatch and opened fire. She fired constantly, peeling back layers of steel. We continued to lift.

We heard a new sound. Heavy blaster fire from outside and the ship started dropping back down.

"On the ground, Jep," Tali said. "Get the girls behind the crates. They might still try to come down and clean up."

I pulled the clump of girls over to a more defensible position and held my nano-blade in front of us defensively. I would die before I allowed anyone to get to these girls, Jenny or not.

The ship settled on the ground with a final bump.

We waited an hour before the hold door opened. I repositioned myself so I was between the door and the girls. The youngest, whose name ironically was Grace, held my hand behind my back.

We heard a commanding voice. "This is Puskar Police, everyone on the ground. Hands behind your heads."

I looked to Tali. She punched Jep in the kidneys again and he fell in a heap. She gave me a sly smile and then kneeled down, placing her hands behind her head. I did the same.

FINALE

"Natalia Liszt! I shoulda known you were involved in this." Half a dozen police in black armored suits entered the cargo bay in a synchronized dance. Long-barreled blasters were pulled snugly against their cheeks and tight against their shoulders. The speaker was a lanky man, not armored, but wearing jeans and a clean white short-sleeved shirt with pockets on both sides. He was tanned and very muscular.

"Polk. You guys sure got here fast," Tali replied. I wasn't sure if she was serious or not. We had been on the ground for better than an hour, cooped up and wondering what was going on.

Polk must not have been clear on what she meant either.

"Seriously? It's not like we didn't have seven other decks to clear."

Tali seemed to have a knack for pushing buttons.

"Easy big fella," she said. "Any chance we can stand up? This level is clear and you're frightening the girls."

"Lieutenant, take the stiff on the ground into custody and clear the rest of this level."

Wordlessly, the armored team spread out and worked their way around the containers. One of them broke off from the team and pulled Jep's arms behind his back. Jep howled in pain as his previously dislocated shoulder was wrenched around. White zip ties were pulled onto his wrists.

"Okay Liszt, you can get up." Polk walked over to us. He wore a brown belt around his waist with a holster hung on it. A white handled blaster pistol sat in it comfortably.

"My sister," I said as he approached. "Jennifer. Did you find her?"

He looked appraisingly at me. "Come again?"

"My sister, she was here. Did you find her?"

"Don't think so, ma'am. Not unless she was regular crew. We have two women in custody. One really old and one my age."

"No. She's only sixteen."

"Well. You'll need to come down to the station and we'll get all this sorted out."

"They took her," a voice behind me said.

I turned around to find the littlest girl in the group had stepped forward. Her big brown eyes were smudged with tears and her clothes were filthy. She let go of the hand of an older girl and moved toward me. My heart broke seeing her in such poor condition. I dropped to my knees and held my arms out. She climbed into my arms.

"What is it, Grace? Do you know what happened to Jenny?"

"They took her."

"Do you remember when they took her, sweetie?"

"Not really. It's so dark."

"Were you on the ground when they took her?"

"Yes."

Bingo! Jenny was on Puskar Stellar.

"Thank you, you've been very brave."

"Do I get to go home now?"

"We'll get you home, kiddo." Polk had walked up behind me. His previously commanding voice was soft.

I stood up and turned to him. "I want to help."

"I get that, but it's not up to me. I'll be doing the investigation, but Family Services will ultimately be responsible for their disposition. Believe me, we'll do everything we can. When we're finished, I can put you in touch with the case worker. Before that, I have some questions that need answers."

"Can I at least stay here with them until Family Services arrive?"

"They're already here. Agent Pilzner caught their case and he knows his way around the block on reintegration." I just stared at him. He made it sound so normal - almost sterile. I could feel my face flush.

"Hey, look," His voice was soft again, no longer a cop giving instructions. "I don't mean anything by it."

A chubby man broke in. "Detective Polk. I see you're now the one in need of a rescue." The man was almost completely bald and had more than one chin. Where Polk was chiseled and clean, Agent Pilzner was soft and rumpled. He gave a warm smile and held his hand out. I had no option but to shake it.

"Terrible thing these girls are going through. We'd love to have your help. It'd do the girls some good to see you once they get cleaned up. Help bring some closure. Would that work?"

"How'd you know?" I asked. He hadn't been anywhere near Polk and me when the conversation started.

"What, that you wanted to get into it with Detective Polk? It's human nature, Miss …"

"Dontal. Celina Dontal."

"You're being protective. It's a basic instinct. Good people want to protect the innocent. Maybe you could introduce me to your new friends? It would go a long way to transferring some of that trust you've established."

I looked guiltily at Polk. He shook his head at me and chuckled. We both knew we were being handled by a pro and I, for one, appreciated it.

Pilzner got right to business and approached the girls. His team spread out, wrapped them in soft blankets, and sheltered them from the active investigation. They were slowly extricated from the scene with a minimum of fuss.

Polk was the only member of his team left in the hold and with all of the girls gone and loaded onto a transport, he waved Tali and me over.

"What in the heck were you doing, Liszt? Do you have a death wish? You should have called us in on this."

"It all happened too quickly," Tali replied.

"Bullshit. You could have dialed us in."

"Okay. You're right. I wasn't expecting this to go south, but I have to admit I had a feeling about it. Next time, I'll give you a heads up."

"Too easy. What're you angling for?"

If Tali didn't have Polk's full attention before, she certainly did now.

"You wound me."

"Out with it."

"There's a missing girl."

"What do you mean?"

"That's why we're here. We had a tip that another girl was on the ship."

"The girl you mentioned earlier? What kind of tip? Frak Tali, you have to give us this information when you get it. This is what we do!"

"Seriously Steve, we got the information at lunch and the ship landed an hour later. We didn't have time."

"I don't suppose that information came from Berta Coffman?"

"Bit."

"Bit?"

"Berta goes by Bit, and yes, we got the information from her. She's creative but very rarely wrong."

"Yeah. You can add persuasive to that list. She rang every comm at SWAT and forwarded the video of the slave pens. She could go to jail for hijacking secure comms like that."

"That gonna be a problem?" Tali asked.

"No. Witnessing a crime in progress like that with young girls, the biggest problem we had was stopping the entire department from coming. So what about this other girl?"

"The girl we're looking for is Celina's younger sister. She was on the ship when it landed."

"Celina? As in …" Polk looked at me and then back at Tali. "Why is it always so hard when you're involved, Liszt? So why are you telling me this now?"

"You have trust issues, Polk."

"Agreed."

"We need to find her. I'm guessing they had someplace for her to go if they took her off right away. They must have had a buyer lined up."

My veins turned to ice and my heart hammered in my chest. I was about to be sick.

"I know who."

Polk and Tali both turned to me at the same time and asked, "Who?"

"Alexander Boyarov. He's not dead. It's him. I know it. He said he'd get to her first."

"Can't be," Tali replied.

"How sure are you?" I asked.

"Who's Boyarov?" Polk interrupted.

"Wait." Tali held her hand up to Polk.

Open priority comm Jordy Keltie.

"Hey, I'm with Polk. Remember the other night, you cleaned up after dinner. What'd you run into?"

I couldn't hear the other side of the conversation.

"You sure? Okay, thanks."

"It might be Boyarov," Tali replied.

"Cleaned up after dinner? Do I want to know? Who's Boyarov?" Polk asked.

"You most definitely don't want to know and it's a long story."

"I'm all ears."

"Lena, it's really your story to tell." Tali looked at me.

I gave it to him straight. Everything from my parent's deaths to being taken prisoner on the Red Houzi base.

"I wish that was the first time I'd heard a story like that, Celina. For what it's worth, I'm sorry." Polk's eyes were soft and glistened. "We can launch a city-wide Trojan search. Do you have any video?"

"Yes," Tali answered. "Bit can forward it to you."

"What's a Trojan search?" I asked.

"We have the capability to require all AI's in the city to do facial matching for the next forty eight hours as long as those AI's are not inside a building. We also scan all satellite and building vids. We aren't allowed to look for criminals with all that, but we can look for missing children. She shows her face for more than three seconds outside or through a window and we'll drop a tactical squad on her location in less than five minutes. Give me a sec to set it up."

Polk stepped away from us to arrange for the search.

"What do you want to do, Lena?" Tali asked.

"I have to talk to Alexander. I'll trade myself for her."

"Not gonna happen."

"It has to. He'll kill her. I have money, Tali. At least I have a way to get money. I have eight crates of high value property, has to be worth at least fifty or sixty thousand. You could get Jenny set up with that money. Please. You have to help me."

"He'll kill you both."

"She'll die without me."

"I get that."

Polk rejoined us so we had to cut off the conversation.

"The search will be up within a few minutes," he said.

"Let us come by tomorrow for a statement?" Tali asked.

"Anyone else, Liszt, I'd say no. Don't make me regret it."

"You're the best, Polk."

"If we get anything from the Trojan, Ms. Dontal, we'll be in contact."

I hoped I was wrong about how this was going to play out, but knew I wasn't. "Thank you, Detective Polk."

I was surprised by the sheer number of police vehicles that surrounded *Domiva's Grace*. Reporter drone cameras buzzed like angry birds and I started getting pings asking for permission to use my face on news feeds. I told my AI to turn them all down.

"Just keep your head down. Anyone asks, we got trapped in a closet and didn't see anything," Tali said.

We took her bike back to Kathryne's boutique.

I was grateful to get back into normal clothing and out of the stevedore's uniform that smelled so much like the slave pens.

"I've been thinking," I said. "This can't be about revenge. It doesn't add up. He would have had to pay for Jenny."

"Right …" Tali answered.

"To me, Jenny is worth everything, but to Alexander, he suddenly wants to pay, what, ten or twenty thousand? Where would he come up with that kind of money? And surely not just to get me back. I was half dead when I finally got away from him, hardly worth that."

"I'm not sure where you're going with this."

"He's after something. Pirates don't do stuff for revenge, unless it's easy to get away with. He would have had to borrow that money, which means he's expecting a quick payoff."

"The crates," Tali said.

"Yes. The crates. They're worth two to three times what he paid for Jenny."

"Interesting."

"We make a trade. Me and the crates for Jenny. Then you save me once Jenny's safe."

"You're just determined to get yourself killed."

"No. I'm determined to save Jenny. I don't want to die, but if that's the cost, then so be it."

"I think I've got this. Here's the plan ..."

With a plan in hand, everything depended on me. Hopefully I hadn't misjudged Alexander.

Establish comm with Alexander Boyarov.

"What? So now you want to talk? Block my call, you crazy ..."

"Where is she, Alexander?" I cut him off, wanting to avoid a rant.

"Talk to your sister. Tell her what we have planned for her," Alexander said.

"Cel? Is that you?"

"Jenny, are you hurt?"

"I'm okay. I'm so sorry. You were gone and I didn't know what to do. They kept me in a cage, Cel. I'm scared. He says he's going to hurt me."

I tried to reassure her, but Alexander cut in. "Got that Dontal? Come on down to the ship and I'll spare your sister."

"Bull," I replied.

"I have your sister. You sure you want to play this game? Scream for your sister, Jenny."

I heard Jenny scream and hot tears rolled down my cheeks.

"Stop it Alexander, you've made your point."

"I don't think I have. Maybe I need to break her in."

"Knock it off. You aren't going to do anything of the sort." I hoped I was right.

"You really want to test that?"

"I have the crates. Let's make it a simple trade. All eight crates for Jenny. You already have the ship."

"How do you know that?"

"You think I'm stupid? You guys don't actually lay low." I gambled.

"Okay, bring the crates to the ship and I'll let your sister go."

"No."

"What?"

"No. If I bring the crates, there's no way you'll let her go. I'll be on the roof of that building where you tried to kill me. You bring Jenny and I'll bring half of the crates. Once Jenny leaves with my friend, I'll take you to the other cases."

"You stupid bitch, I have your family. That's not how this is going down. You bring the cases and you hope I don't kill her because of your stupidity."

"No."

"Scream for your sister."

Once again I could hear Jenny screaming. I muted. "I can't take it, Tali. He's hurting her."

"You take this deal, he'll kill you and do unspeakable things to your sister. He can't really hurt her. If this falls through, he'll sell her and she's worth nothing if she's damaged. Don't be weak, Lena. You have to be strong for Jenny!"

I thought about it and cussed. I didn't know if I could go through with this. I unmuted. "You know my terms, call me back once you're serious about dealing." I terminated comms. It was the hardest thing I'd ever done.

Unblock Alexander Boyarov's communications.

We sat in Kathryne's shop, staring at each other. If Alexander's temper got the worst of him I'd made a critical mistake and Jenny would pay for it.

Incoming comm from Alexander Boyarov. I connected.

"Are you ready to do this?" I asked.

"You're coming with me. The deal is the cases and you, and your friend gets your sister. You bring one friend. That's it."

"I won't tell you where the other cases are if you harm anyone."

"One hour," he said.

"We'll be there."

"If I see more than one other person, I'll kill your sister, then your friend, then you. Got it?"

I hung up. I called the storage unit where I had half of the crates stored and instructed them to deliver them to Kathryne's Boutique. Tali arranged to get a small runabout, big enough to carry us and the crates.

"We have to make one stop on the way," Tali said.

"Okay."

Forty-five minutes later we were on the roof. Alexander was nowhere to be found. We waited fifteen minutes before two larger passenger runabouts buzzed the top of the building. Tali and I had to duck.

One of the vehicles landed at the opposite end of the roof and its back door opened. Jenny was sitting in the seat, held in place by Alexander.

The other vehicle continued to slowly orbit the roof. I couldn't tell who was in that vehicle until the door opened and a man I didn't recognize aimed a large blaster rifle at me. Olav Peetre, the pirate who had been responsible for originally abducting me sat next to him.

Open comm with Alexander Boyarov. I held my right hand up high. "I have a dead man's switch, Alexander. The crates and I are set to blow if you pull anything."

"Oh, you are getting fancy. Okay, we'll play nice."

"Let Jenny out and have her walk toward my vehicle."

He pushed Jenny out.

"Walk over to me, Dontal," Alexander demanded.

"Not until Jenny is in the other vehicle."

Alexander stepped out and took a handful of Jenny's soiled robe. Pulling her along, he walked straight to me.

"You almost had me. Nice idea on the dead man's switch." Alexander punched me in the gut hard, and grabbed my hand as I bent over in agony.

"No, no, let's not drop that. You got no play here. You drop it and you'll kill Jenny. You lose. I have to say I underestimated you, but you just aren't quite as smart as you think. You shouldn't have let your sister near the explosives."

Alexander looked at the circling vehicle. "Shoot the extra."

I watched as the man opened fire on Tali's position - only Tali was no longer there.

"Find her!" Alexander screamed.

"Let her go! She isn't part of this."

"Yeah, whatever."

We watched as the vehicle swooped around, looking for Tali.

"You have less than a minute to get out of here, Alexander." I said, hoping it wasn't a bluff.

"You called the police?"

"No, but they're coming all the same."

"Hmm. Well, I guess you screwed us all then." Alexander turned and started to drag Jenny away.

I couldn't let Jenny go. I wouldn't let her be taken into the life I escaped. I dropped the dead man's switch - it was just a decoy anyway. I jumped on Jenny and wrapped her up with my arms. There was no way Alexander would be able to drag us both back.

I thought I heard sirens. So did Alexander. He released Jenny's robe as I drug her down to the ground.

"Shoot them both and get out of here." Alexander said into his comm. He took off at a run toward his parked vehicle.

The other vehicle stopped its pursuit of Tali and swung toward Jenny and me. I rolled protectively over on top of her, trying to place my body in line with the shooter. Alexander was almost to his vehicle when I saw him stumble. A bright red cloud appeared next to his head and he fell to the ground, no longer moving.

Closing my eyes, I braced for shots that never came. Instead, I heard a loud explosion and felt a pressure wave press into my back. I covered Jenny's head with my arms and looked up to see the flaming remains of the second vehicle as it lost altitude and fell out of view.

"Lena!" Tali yelled as she sprinted to me. I had no idea where she had come from. She slid across the pebbles of the roof, wrapping her arms around Jenny and me.

Sirens were blaring, closing in on us.

"Tell me you're both okay!" she yelled over the noise.

I felt Jenny moving beneath me.

"Jenny?"

"Celina?"

I helped her to a seated position and inspected her. She was filthy, but I couldn't see any blood. She wrapped her arms around me and Tali hugged us both.

Channel One comm, Tali said. "All clear. Kelti, Reehl, get out now, locals en route. No friendly casualties. I say again everybody is UP."

"Where were they?" I asked.

"Look over there." Tali nodded in the direction of a building two kilometers away.

"That far?"

"It's okay to be impressed, just don't say it to Jordy. He's already hard enough to get along with."

I looked at her in disbelief and then we heard a familiar amplified voice. "Everyone down on the ground."

I helped Jenny get on her knees and put her hands behind her head. "It's okay, Jenny. It's the good guys."

Polk approached, shaking his head. "Twice in a day!? You gotta frakking be kidding me.

ABOUT THE AUTHOR

Jamie McFarlane has been writing short stories and telling tall tales for several decades. With a focus that only a bill collector could inspire, he has finally relented to recording some of his most of requested stories.

During the day Jamie can be found at his home, writing in front of a neglected fire, with his two cats both conveniently named Dragon. When not writing, Jamie can be found at the local pub sharing his stories with any who will listen.

Thank you for reading. I'm so glad you enjoyed it. Please consider using one or more of the following links to learn about additional books in the Privateer Tales series or just to stay in contact with Jamie.

Blog and Website: fickledragon.com

Facebook: facebook.com/jamiemcfarlaneauthor

Twitter: twitter.com/privateertales

Made in the USA
Charleston, SC
05 June 2014